Praise for *Nights When*

"A deeply affecting portrait of one fami[...]
the toll that the American Dream takes [...]

"How does a family find its footing after it leaves home for good?. . . .
Rendered in a series of quick brush strokes, as if in a Raymond Carver
story . . . [and] seen from the shifting perspectives of mother, father,
daughter, and son—each fully, empathetically rendered . . . this novel
reminds us what it's like navigating a foreign country. . . . Much to
admire." —*The New York Times Book Review*

"A tender, spiky family saga about love in all its mysterious incarnations.
Simon Han is a wonderfully adventurous and sensitive writer."
—Lorrie Moore, author of *A Gate at the Stairs* and *Birds of America*

"Entirely worth the investment. . . . Han's expansive sympathy and twi-
light lyricism make *Nights When Nothing Happened* a poignant study of the
immigrant experience. This is an author who understands on a profound
level the way past trauma interacts with the pressures of assimilation to
disrupt a good night's sleep, even a life." —*The Washington Post*

"Searing . . . Han asks a timeless yet urgent question: Is it possible to feel
truly safe in a place that wasn't made for you?" —*Time*

"In this beautiful, unsettling novel, Simon Han captures the state of being
awake and yet asleep, of belonging and yet not, of waiting for the moment
when the world opens up. He reveals how fragile we are, and what it takes
to survive. An unbelievable debut."
—Kevin Wilson, author of *Nothing to See Here*

"[A] dazzling debut . . . In this subtle but deeply felt story, Han elegantly
takes aim at suburban racism, generational trauma, and the secrets we
keep from one another in order to stay afloat." —*Esquire*

"*Nights When Nothing Happened* is very much about the private, shadowy
parts of ordinary lives, but Han's evocative writing is anything but ordinary. . . . A brief novel best read slowly, so one can savor the resonance
and originality Han wrings from the quotidian. . . . Han's gift at zeroing
in on matters of the conflicted heart is its own reward." —*NPR*

"Absolutely luminous. Han weaves the transience of suburbia between the
highs and lows of a family saga, illustrating what a parent owes a child,

what a child owes their parents, and what simply cannot be repaid. His novel shocks, awes, and delights."

—Bryan Washington, author of *Memorial*

"Han writes with sublime suspense. . . . [He] has a keen ability to write of not only the subtleties of the disappointments and loneliness that can be found within families, but also of how the specific and often unsubtle threats of American oppression, especially against perceived outsiders, can seep into the immigrant's most intimate familial relationships."

—*San Francisco Chronicle*

"Elegant, elegiac . . . Han's creation of the Chengs is remarkable for his refusal to make them into heroic figures. He is bold enough to portray them, with great understanding and tenderness, as no one other than the striving, anxious, imperfect humans that they are." —*The Dallas Morning News*

"Achingly tender and emotionally devastating. A stunning debut that will stay with me." —Charles Yu, author of *Interior Chinatown*

"Han excels at depicting bright, bland Plano, a suburb of 'sprinkler-fed grass,' 'vanilla-scented pine cones,' and 'oven mitts and motion sensors.' Even in carefully planned, hermetically sealed Plano, there's no controlling the cascade of events that ensue when a wild child is unleashed in a community that does not understand her family." —*Star Tribune*

"Outstanding . . . the suspense building is masterful . . . It is not a happy family story, but it is nonetheless a satisfying one, full of introspection, the fragility created by self-doubt realistically depicted."

—*Southern Review of Books*

"Simon Han explores the desire to belong—to a marriage, a family, a community, a country. *Nights When Nothing Happened* is about how we use words and silences to connect and to wound, and how we make sacrifices for those we love. It broke my heart and gave me hope, all at the same time." —Angie Kim, author of *Miracle Creek*

"Brings texture, nuance, and subtlety to the reductionist condescension of the 'model minority' trope." —*The Millions*

"Han displays incredible range as a novelist, oscillating between honest, almost tangibly real scenes, opaque dreams, and refractive memories. . . . [His] prose is vivid yet restrained, and his characters are multidimensional and alive. Emotionally resonant and packed with nuance, this is an exemplary debut novel." —*BookPage* (starred review)

Nights When

NOTHING

Happened

◑

SIMON HAN

RIVERHEAD BOOKS   *New York*

RIVERHEAD BOOKS
An imprint of Penguin Random House LLC
penguinrandomhouse.com

Riverhead and the R colophon are registered
trademarks of Penguin Random House LLC.

Grateful acknowledgment is made to reprint an excerpt from "Epistle"
from *Rose* by Li-Young Lee. Copyright © 1986 by Li-Young Lee.
Reprinted with the permission of The Permissions Company,
LLC on behalf of BOA Editions, Ltd., boaeditions.org]

The Library of Congress has catalogued the Riverhead hardcover edition as follows:

Names: Han, Simon, author.
Title: Nights when nothing happened / Simon Han.
Description: New York : Riverhead Books, 2020.
Identifiers: LCCN 2020003942 (print) | LCCN 2020003943 (ebook) |
ISBN 9780593086056 (hardcover) | ISBN 9780593086070 (ebook)
Classification: LCC PS3608.A69696 N54 2020 (print) |
LCC PS3608.A69696 (ebook) | DDC 813/.6--dc23
LC record available at https://lccn.loc.gov/2020003942
LC ebook record available at https://lccn.loc.gov/2020003943

First Riverhead hardcover edition: November 2020
First Riverhead trade paperback edition: November 2021
Riverhead trade paperback ISBN: 9780593086063

Printed in Canada
1st Printing

Book design by Cassandra Garruzzo

For Chanhee

But a stranger in a strange land, he is no one;
men know him not—and to know not is to care
not for.

BRAM STOKER, *DRACULA*

Before it all gets wiped away, let me say,
there is wisdom in the slender hour
which arrives between two shadows.

LI-YOUNG LEE, "EPISTLE"

Nights When

NOTHING

Happened

1

Jack Cheng knew about protection. He knew who gave it and who needed it, and he knew that he was the one who'd found his sister curled around the toilet one night, sleep-walking into the swinging kitchen door another night, and that was a calling.

Most nights had limped along since his parents began putting Annabel to sleep in her own room instead of theirs. When sleep finally came to them, they would snore the way kings and queens with servants to adjust their pillows all night long snore, dreaming dreams that were not anyone's right to interrupt. At an hour when the house held its breath and waited for something to happen, Jack stayed up and read books in which characters died, literally, of fright. The sound of a leaf scraping across the sidewalk could draw him downstairs in socks until he reached hardwood. Then, realizing that his sister was still safe upstairs, he would stand in the dark before his mother's favorite sheepskin rug and imagine that the rattling and scratching he was hearing behind the walls came from beavers, though he had never seen a beaver and confused them with raccoons.

Late one night in November, a steady pounding woke him up. He lay under the covers for some time, remembering that his mother had not been home when he went to bed, and wondering if she had come back from work or he had dreamed it. Downstairs, he found the front door open to the street. Had the calling moved beyond toilets and kitchens? He wandered outside without slapping on shoes, his mind still muddled with dream sounds. On the sidewalk, he skirted a pile of dog shit and an issue of *The Dallas Morning News* still wrapped in yellow film. The houses on both sides of Plimpton Court stood like tombs, each split down the middle by a cobbled pathway, one fledgling oak or elm on either side. In front of two houses, Christmas lights already spiraled up the thin trunks and framed the eaves, the work of professionals. From a balcony, an inflatable Santa raised a mitten in his direction and did not lower it. Jack had made a habit during the day of crouching by the window in the piano room and waving hello back, which always sent Annabel into fits of giggles. It had not occurred to him until now that the Santa could be waving good-bye. He kept on, avoiding its eyes.

He found the first of Annabel's glow-in-the-dark slippers on the Brenners' front lawn. Crouching down, he brushed grass clippings from the plush cotton. He pressed a hand on a sunken patch of grass. He pressed here, he pressed there. A strange thought came to him: maybe the heartbeat he was feeling did not belong to him but to the grass, and to the earthworms slithering beneath. If he followed the trail of heartbeats between the Brenners' and the Driscolls' he would find the other slipper. He rushed forward, staying low and close to a brown fence at the corner of Plimpton and Main that still gave off paint fumes. There was no time to pull up his socks. The cracks between the planks glowed a phosphorescent blue. A swimming pool. There was something about a lighted swimming pool at midnight that reminded Jack of murder and intrigue.

A car passed on Main Street, its headlights flashing through the fence and illuminating the leaves floating in the pool. His sister could be drifting toward this vacant stretch of road where high schoolers tore through in trucks with wheels bigger than her, blazing a shortcut out to Sheridan. He followed the path he imagined her taking, between houses and down alleyways, until he reached the sewage creek that cut through the community. During the summer, he remembered, the feet and underside of a duck had bobbed there for days. On the grass that sloped up from the creek, he spotted the glow of the other slipper.

His sister stood a few yards away, on the bridge that overlooked the creek. Under a towering steel streetlight, she swayed slightly. Her head was lifted, and a white glow bloomed from her neck, up to the stretch of baby fat under her chin. Her eyes were closed, as if she were basking in the pool of light. If Jack did not know better, he would have thought a spaceship had beamed her down to earth. He sidled beside her, a slipper in each hand. He was Annabel's protector, but sometimes he did not know what to do with his hands.

"Hear me in there? Knock-knock?"

Annabel blinked. "You found me, Daddy."

A few dead crickets still clung to the lamp. The stink of the summer's crickets had carried through the end of fall, and perhaps would last through a winter that never arrived. It was no wonder he'd thought American air to be unsafe. In those early years in Plano, Jack had held his breath around diapers and hospitals and graveyards and urinals and police stations and fertilizer and roadkill and cameras and his father.

"Daddy," his sister said.

"Okay," he said.

"Daddy. Daddy. Daddy. Dad—"

"I heard you."

Now, that call again. That *Breathe, Jack*. That *Take your sister away, Jack*. Away from the light. Away from the image of dead crickets falling, as faintly as the first snow in China, into her little mouth. It was a new day, and they needed to go back: to the sprinkler-fed grass, the potted mums, the vanilla-scented pinecones that would remind him, in any season, of this place he'd lived in Texas. *Take her back, Jack, take her back.*

This fall of 2003, Jack was eleven and his sister five, the span between them never changing, though he felt that it should. Six years contained an entire life. They equaled, he reminded himself, the number of years that he'd lived in China. The more years Jack had accumulated in Plano, the more he'd shed of that first life, and in the days before Annabel began sleepwalking, what he recalled most clearly was his own daydreaming, perched by the fourth-story window of his grandparents' apartment in Tianjin.

His earliest memories were of looking down at older buildings, while his later ones were of looking up: craning his neck toward condos and offices that sprouted in a matter of months, crammed in staggered formation so that where one building ended in the skyline, the next began. They bled into his view of the muddy Hai River, the uniformed street sweepers, the market from which every few days his grandparents wheeled groceries home. There went the older buildings, the greenhouses growing like hair on their roofs. There went green itself.

The older and stronger Jack became, the more he saw the wobbly legs that held up his city. Beyond the high-rises were the cobblestoned streets flanked by forts and villa-style houses, complete with red tile roofs that Italian invaders had erected. The giant cross on a French cathedral bore down on pedestrians, slinging sun into their eyes. A Japanese house with manicured gardens had once been home to the last emperor of China, a traitor who'd sold out his country to the enemy. There were German barracks, British hotels, Austro-Hungarian mansions. Jack could not point on his grandparents' globe to where any of these invaders were from, but he could picture their faces, grinning demonically in the water swirling in Lǎolao's mop pail, or in the faded brown rings at the bottom of Lǎoye's teacup. With a swing of his sword, he knocked back bowls of their congealing soy milk, stabbed the heart of the electric fan that made the summers bearable. Lǎolao and Lǎoye saved their heads by ducking. They cursed the day they'd bought him the cheap plaything. What did it matter that Jack was defending them? They cared only about minor hazards like crossing a street, ordering Jack to hold on to them. When he shattered a vase made in Belgium, they fought back. Their palms cut deeper than swords; it hurt to sit down at the dinner table. Sometimes they picked up the phone and, instead of bickering with the milkman, reported him to his parents.

His parents. His parents in America. Jack saw them as they were in the photograph that leaned against a tin of sunflower seeds on the cabinet. His mother's hair pulled back by a clip, a large vein visible on her forehead. Her eyes narrow and level, as if she were concentrating fiercely on not dropping the baby in her lap. She never scolded Jack as harshly as Lǎolao and Lǎoye demanded. *Do the shoes I had Dàjiu buy for you still fit?* she would ask. *Are you eating the pork I told Lǎolao to cook? Have you read the English book I asked Èrjiu to bring from school?* When his mother's words grew tiresome, he used his grandparents as models to imagine, on the other end of the receiver, her moving mouth: Lǎoye's long, drooping jaw lifted and chiseled into a robust square, Lǎolao's puckered lips pulled into a taut line instead of a perpetually surprised *O*. His father was harder to construct because he did not come from Lǎolao and Lǎoye—did not come from anyone or anywhere, it seemed, his past in the countryside muffled by the low voices other adults used when talking about him, saying things like *those people* and *places like that*. In the photograph leaning against the tin, Jack's father wore a suit so big his shoulders appeared inflated, though his dress shirt underneath was too small, the collar unbuttoned to give his thick neck room to breathe. While baby Jack and his mother looked straight at the camera, his father stood beside the chair, staring off at a different angle, which Jack once projected with a ruler to about five centimeters from the upper-right corner of the frame.

"You're a damned rascal!" Lǎolao said.

"You'll make us die early!" Lǎoye said.

"Time to send you to America!" Lǎolao said.

"You think we're bluffing?" Lǎoye said.

His grandparents, for all their embellishments, eventually reached a moment of truth. They dragged Jack onto a bus to the Beijing airport, where they delivered him into the trust of two family friends, childless āyís whose faces he would forget within months. At the security check, he looked back at his grandparents and realized that they had become undeniably, irrevocably old. As Lǎolao waved from a distance, he could see the redness of her palm and the swelling of her fingers; perhaps all the times he'd squeezed her wrist crossing streets had cut off the blood in her hands from the rest of her body. Lǎoye's shoulders hunched forward, and without a cane he teetered at the edge of an imagined cliff, helpless in the midst of people who rolled their luggage past him, not knowing how easy it would be to knock him over. Jack had made his grandparents frail, too frail to come with him. When they turned their faces away and dabbed their eyes with a single shared handkerchief, he wondered if they regretted sending him away. Maybe it wasn't all his fault for being a dǎodàngui̯, maybe his leaving was, as he'd been taught to believe, inevitable. He was going to live with his parents, who seemed to him not people so much as a destination he did not want to visit.

But he would. He would have to. In the plane, the āyí to his left asked him if he was as eager as she was to try airplane food for the first time, and the āyí to his right let him in on a rumor about the otherworldly flushing speeds of the toilets. When the plane crawled backward from the terminal, the two women smiled and reached past him, their fingers meeting in the space behind his head. One āyí stroked the side of the other's hand with her thumb, and the other extended a finger to tickle a vein under the wrist, and in the glimpses Jack allowed himself to take, their faces carried another message, shrouded in a language he could not access, lips that moved with words he could not hear.

Then from the ceiling, a voice spoke through warbled static, addressing the passengers first in Mandarin, then in English. *Please direct your attention to the flight attendants for an important safety demonstration.* Outside, the people wearing orange vests and waving orange sticks disappeared, replaced by a runway dressed up with meticulously spaced lights. *There are several emergency exits on this aircraft.* Following the voice's instructions, Jack pulled out the laminated card in front of him, on which cartoon people encountered endless terrors but faced them without fear, without any feeling at all. *Remember to secure your oxygen mask first before assisting your child.* Where was he going, that the journey there could be so treacherous? After the smiling flight attendants began to blow into tubes on their life vests, Jack leaned forward and hugged his legs in the bracing position of the cartoon people. He did not move when one āyí placed her hand on his back and moved it in steady circles. *We remind you not to tamper with, disable, or destroy the smoke detectors.* He stared down, ignoring the āyí's hand and focusing on the card he'd dropped. In the last panel there was a boy, a smaller version of the cartoon man behind him. He wanted nothing more than to whoosh down the giant yellow slide with them, his arms pointed stiffly forward, halfway to solid ground.

He would take other flights, hear other safety demonstrations. But five years later, on the first day of middle school, when his teacher stood at the front of the room and ordered twenty-three sixth graders not to say *kill*, it was that voice Jack would remember, arriving over warbled static, and the English that followed. That feeling of being in a cartoon.

"Do not say *die*," his English teacher said. "Do not say *stab, murder, choke, shoot,* or *bomb*. Especially *bomb*." Mr. Morris rolled up his sleeves. Veins snaked up his arms and under his shirt, like those of bodybuilders or the elderly—Mr. Morris could pass for either. "Never say *bomb*."

It was August. Jack sat at his new desk-chair, not sure what to do with his legs. The formation of rows and columns left him feeling exposed. And girls—some wore perfume. Scents welled from below their necklines, calling back the candied fruit that he'd once swiped from the street vendors outside his grandparents' apartment. He had not thought about the taste of glazed strawberries and pineapples and shānzhā for so long, the way he'd slid them up and off the skewer with his teeth. And the vendors, the spittle in their mouths as they raised their newspapers to whack him.

The girl in front of him turned around, the end of her ponytail whipping the top of his hand, to pass back a stack of letters, each addressed to the parents and signed by the principal. On his way to America, Jack remembered, he had carried a letter, too. A letter *from* his parents. A letter to prove that he belonged to parents, written in English.

"Is *punch* okay?" a boy asked from the back of the classroom.

"You can probably say *punch*," Mr. Morris said.

"What about *assassinate*?"

"*Assassinate* is usually reserved for public figures."

"What about *manslaughter*?"

"*Manslaughter*," Mr. Morris said, as if trying out a name for a newborn. He fingered the swirl of his tie. "Well, *manslaughter* is not a verb. Speaking of verbs."

A voice behind Jack said, "I'm scared." Heads swiveled around, but no one could identify the speaker. Fingers were pointed in opposing directions, giggles shushed. After class, Jack wondered if he had been the speaker. If somehow he hadn't known.

Jack should not have been scared. His parents had decided to live in Plano in order not to be scared. Plano had the lowest crime rate in Texas, highly ranked schools, churches bigger than schools, lighted tennis courts, malls that closed before 9:00 p.m. After he'd joined his parents, his mother had called his grandparents to let them know that he was *here*, he was safe. When a forgetful Lǎolao had asked where *here* was, she said *near Dallas*. Later, when she introduced Jack to their neighbors, she said that he was from *near Beijing*. Jack had wondered then if his homes were not only safe, but imagined.

He did not know, even by middle school, that in the late 1990s this affluent suburb had been dubbed "the heroin capital of America." Nor that in the early '80s, it had been called "the suicide capital of America." Every year, a new wave of residents diluted the collective memory of the city, like fresh customers unwittingly enlisted in a company's rebranding. *Just say no* was as much as his teachers were willing to tell him. No drugs, no suicide, no fights, no sex, no drinking, no depression, no slacking, and now, no saying, *You wanna die?* No more, *I'm gonna kill you.* And though no one had taken those threats seriously before, banning the words morphed them into something serious. Something threatening.

That night, his mother brought the letter to his room. She lay at the foot of the bed, the balls of her feet pressed into the carpet. Lǎoye had talked about how, as a child, she'd walk over the knots of his back. "Should I worry?" she asked.

His mother had always been a bony person, a woman of acute angles and protrusions. In the photograph propped against the tin of sunflower seeds, baby Jack had seemed eager to get off her lap. He had not seen the picture since he'd left, but having his mother near made him want to remember her, the way she'd been when she was far.

"*Mom*," he said.

Jack leaned against the headboard with another of his old *Choose Your Own Adventure* books in his lap. The books were too easy for him, but it was nice to fall asleep before reaching The End. When there were multiple endings in a book, the one he arrived at always left him bereft, though he could not say of what. He lost his page. A few ends of his mother's hair fell over his toes. What would it feel like to touch his mother's face with his feet? A privilege reserved, perhaps, for babies and toddlers, who would grow up unable to remember what it had felt like to touch their mothers' faces with their feet.

Some children graduate to kisses. Like Annabel, who insisted on delivering one hundred each night before sleeping. She'd just started kindergarten at a new Montessori-inspired school, and their parents were using the transition to try to make her sleep in her own room. Was she the reason their parents never kissed each other? Was he? They had probably kissed more when it was only the two of them in Houston. In Tianjin, he'd pictured his parents in America funneling rice into their mouths and swaying to Kenny G and dozing off in front of the TV, but not until Annabel was born had he thought about them kissing. Now his father was across the hall, tucking Annabel in. Surely he'd let her drag out her kisses. *One hundred and two, one hundred and three.* Jack imagined Annabel pulling his father back to bed, her hand clamped around a finger; he imagined his father pretending she was stronger than she was. Once she started crying, he would not be able to leave. It would be another long night. In the morning, Jack would run his hand across the mattress, the dips here and there.

His mother dug her elbows into his bed and pushed herself up. Tomorrow, before Jack or the birds had woken up, she would be gone, and no one in the house would remark on her absence; it had become normal again to start the day without her. Half of his mother was already on its way out of the room. She reached for the fan switch but changed her mind. Her finger hung in the air as if to say, *This is a fan switch. This is a wall.* "Close the fan," she said.

"*Turn off* the fan."

"Good night, jīn gǒu'r."

Gold dog, his mother called him. The *dog* to ensure he'd grow up healthy and strong, a humbling nickname, only she'd added the *gold*. Gold, golden, goldest, she'd say, as if Jack's growing up were a series of escalating adjectives. The woman had not flinched at the bad reports his grandparents had made about him. The boy who'd joined her in this country did not say bad words, let alone banned words. He did not break expensive vases, or steal from poor street vendors. He did not cling to her. He did not dare sleep with her. Here was Jack, a boy who took so little space he might as well still be in Tianjin.

As his mother left the room, he shut his eyes. A few nights later, he would find Annabel lying on her side by the toilet across the hall. She would be sleeping deeply, her arms hugging the toilet's base. Kneeling closer to her, he would spot faint yellow streaks along the tiles, discarded nail clippings. But the bath mat was soft, and as he lifted her head from it he would remember not China but a busy aisle in Home Depot, where his mother had pressed that softness to her face. She'd closed her eyes in the middle of the store, rubbed her cheek from one corner of the mat to the other. Strangers had looked over. He'd assumed then that the mat was for his parents' bathroom, but when they got back, his father brought it upstairs, telling Jack to be careful because Turkish cotton was not easy to wash.

Even after that first night he discovered Annabel in the bathroom, Jack could not say for certain that she was a sleepwalker. People had walked at all hours in Tianjin, the ceiling thumping at three in the morning while a drunk bathed the street in song. Aside from the annual fireworks displays or the occasional air-raid drills, the nights' movements had not stirred him, let alone called to him. Hearing the opening salvo of his grandparents' snoring from the other room was assurance that he could close his eyes. Only here had he come to know about sleepwalkers. He imagined them as the zombies in *The Walking Dead* comics, who weren't called zombies, just walkers. He hadn't thought about where sleepwalkers went after the walking ceased. A sleepwalker who wasn't walking was simply sleeping. But Annabel had started at one place and ended at another and there was a story of the in-between that he wanted to learn, a story available only to him, not even to Annabel.

Late August and early September were the long days of learning. The locker-lined walls of Fillmore Middle School penned him in, while his sister's school, Plano Star Care, shuttled its students on field trips ambitious even for the gifted. During her third week of kindergarten, after a visit to the JFK assassination museum, Annabel used a word she'd never used before: *fascinating*. "They got video," she told their mother as the two of them sat at the kitchen table, tearing the ends off green beans. "Fascinating."

In the adjoining living room, the TV in front of Jack announced the latest scandal in the Catholic Church. Numbers were thrown out. Twelve. Eighty-four. Five hundred and fifty-two. These were scary numbers, the steely eyed commentator stated. Before the commercial break, she promised that they would return to the war coverage.

"He was in the car," Annabel said. "And the car had no roof. And his head went *blam*! Like when Daddy dropped the watermelon. Me and Elsie watched fourteen times."

"Háizi!" his mother said. "Where were your teachers?"

"Around," Annabel said. "And then we went to the Grassy Knoll. That's where the video happened. Elsie told me she saw blood on the road."

Elsie was Annabel's new best friend. A day earlier, his sister had boasted about Elsie's dream to hurl herself from the monkey bars so she could break her arm and get a cast littered with drawings and signatures. His mother shushed her now as she'd shushed her then, but Annabel pressed on. "The head," she said, "the head went *blam-blam-blam*. All the way to China! *Blam!*" She snapped the green beans in half—*blam!*—then in fourths—*blam!*

"Stop!" his mother said, but Jack didn't know if she was talking about the JFK story or the green beans. "*Stop*—wǒde mā ya—*stop!*"

Jack turned around from the couch: his father was draping a giant forearm around Annabel's neck. He had Jack's sister pinned against the chair, his forearm pressing down on her throat as Annabel's hands flailed in the air. His father grinned and Annabel laughed and his mother laughed and the TV commercial behind Jack laughed, too. He should have laughed, laughed at the silly game his father and sister liked to play.

His father brought his arm back to his side. He scratched his ass with his oven mitt. At his photography studio he slung around long-nosed cameras heavier than babies, while at home he sported an apron of Monet's water lilies, nearly small enough to serve as a bib. When he smiled he shut his eyes, lost in some distant pleasant thought. His mother laughed when she was happy and frowned when she was upset, but in the five years

Jack had known his father, mannequin's faces had proven easier to read.

"You got to be scarier!" Annabel said. "It's in the eyes, Daddy!" She stood up on her chair and, without warning, socked their father's belly. *For every action,* Jack had learned, *there is an equal and opposite reaction.* What would it feel like to punch his father in the stomach? When Annabel tired of punching, she plopped back down with the flair of a wounded TV wrestler and plucked the end off a green bean. His mother told her not to put it in her mouth. His father returned to the kitchen, cracking his back on the way. His game was a success. For the time being, Annabel had forgotten about John F. Kennedy's head.

At Jack's school the next day, his safety was not a game. Preparing for a potential intruder was no laughing matter. Lock the classroom door. Close the blinds. Turn off the lights. Coach Becker, his health teacher and a demonstrative door locker, twisted the switch as if in slow motion, which led to a resounding, foreboding *click.* "Push the desks against the door," Coach Becker said. "Sit in the corner. Now." When Marco Martinez tittered, Coach Becker ordered him out into the open center of the classroom, to do thirty-five push-ups. Jack looked on with the rest of the class without saying a word. Marco lived across the street and had beaten Jack in sixteen straight games of Clue, but when it came to push-ups there was no need to count. The boy weighed nearly two Jacks and couldn't get his hips off the ground. He heaved. His eyes, pooled with sweat, implored Coach Becker for mercy. *Kill me*, he must have been thinking. *I want to die!* It was better that Marco wasn't allowed to say it.

When he got home, Jack told Annabel about the drill. "Guess what? We practiced hiding from school shooters. Marco Martinez barfed." She ate his stories up, with the serious fascination children reserve for adults crying in public, or animals mating. "Oh, I never saw a real shooter," she said.

"That's enough," their father said, herding them to the refrigerator for ice cream.

Annabel refused to sleep by herself again that night. To release herself to sleep was to allow Māma and Daddy to abandon her to a dark and dangerous world. One parent tucking her in was no longer enough. Her wailing reminded Jack of his first months in America, when his father's nightmares had kept him awake. They lived in a one-bedroom in East Plano then, an apartment half the size of his grandparents'. Think of it like another plane ride, his mother told him. A means to an end, not a place to call home. But from the mattress in the living room, Jack could spy, past the bent plastic of a window blind, switchgrass taller than him. Beyond that, the illuminated sign of a dry cleaner that had been in business for more years than he'd been alive. There was a story in the loose spring by his foot, the stain under one corner of the mattress. A chapter he was living, even as his parents prepared for the next one. When his father sometimes yelled out from his parents' bedroom in the middle of the night, he did not utter a word, in any language, that Jack could understand. He could only hear his mother on the other side of the door, pleading for him to stop.

Now Jack left the door to his room open and listened as his mother assured Annabel, the way she'd assured Jack in those first months, that there was nothing to see. Nothing under Annabel's bed, nothing in the closet, nothing in the mirror, nothing in Daddy's hands, nothing in Daddy's head. Annabel pecked a cheek that was nothing more than a surface for her lips to touch. She took a gulp of nothing air. When she finally stopped crying, there was no sound of footsteps shuffling back downstairs. No reason for his parents to take their leave. The only way Jack could imagine their bodies fitting on his sister's bed was with his mother's elbows prodding Annabel and half of his father's body splayed over the side.

The second time Annabel sleepwalked was a night in October. A night when the dark, mirrorless castle of Count Dracula materialized outside Jack's bedroom door and past the narrow corridor where the floorboards sometimes creaked. One wrong step and he could end up swallowed, like the screaming pony in *The Hound of the Baskervilles*, into the quicksand of the Great Grimpen Mire. A night like any other night, in any other place.

A light percussive noise rang from downstairs. Jack lowered his *Dracula* paperback. Again, he heard the sound: a muffled thump, followed by a clattering. As he went down the stairs, the sound persisted. In the unlit kitchen, Annabel stood next to an open drawer, just tall enough to see the chopsticks and porcelain spoons, the forks and knives that caught a glint of moonlight. Her head lolled toward her chest, and her long, shadowy hair fell over her eyes.

"Annabel?" he said. "Why are you up?"

Without acknowledging him, she slammed the drawer shut. The utensils rattled.

"Where's Mom and Dad?"

She walked across the island to a far drawer he had never thought to open. It was stuffed full of coupons. First Uncle, who'd visit Lǎolao and Lǎoye from the coast of Binhai, had told Jack how his parents were trying to save money in America, so Jack could join them as soon as possible. His mother, First Uncle said, busied herself in labs, tinkering with metals and the invisible particles that circled like galaxies inside them. She could knock the particles into one another and create a current of electricity that carried her voice across an ocean and into his ear to say how much she missed him. His father, meanwhile, was one of *those people*, raised by fānfū parents in the far-off mountains who did not know how to care for him the way Lǎolao and Lǎoye cared for Jack's mother, but he did his best. While his mother worked, his father probably drove from the Statue of Liberty to the Golden Gate Bridge, not for pleasure but to take photographs so his son could see what he saw, so his son could come to America already American.

Jack knew First Uncle, a low-level engineer himself, had a not-so-secret flair for the dramatic, and with every passing year that his parents did not call for him, the more he saw his uncle's stories as adversarial to his own. Jack was not a sleek car behind the window of a dealership, waiting for the day that its owners would have the money and time to devote to it. Let his parents go on living in their subsidized rental in Houston, his mother's feet tucked under his father's thighs as they snipped ads for frozen food and paper towels and underwear from the weekly inserts. Their son, Jack decided, could not be so easily bought and reacquired. He was in China because he belonged there.

In America, Jack had learned that he had been right not to trust First Uncle's stories. His mother wore cardigans and skirt suits to work, not white coats and goggles. She was weighed down by big assignments that she did not explain, making tiny microchips that he could crush with his foot as if they were tortilla chips. If his father went outside, it was mainly to tend the Red River lilies that dotted the entryway of their house, the camellias that stuck to the bushes like toilet paper. In the family photo albums, his father had taken the occasional shot of Plano—red columns like futuristic smokestacks rising out of a Cinemark theater; a lone cul-de-sac of eight or nine houses, the sidewalks still under construction, in the middle of fallow farmland—but no Empire State Building, no Hollywood etched into a mountain. Jack could no longer imagine his parents lounging around, cutting coupons. Even when he'd first met them, they'd studied baby catalogs, suspicious of sales. If a crib was 50 percent off, something was wrong with it. The coupons had to be older than Annabel, Jack thought now. When she shut the drawer, a couple of them flew into the air and drifted onto the linoleum.

"What's going on?" he said.

Annabel brushed past him. She walked with intention, in the direction of the playroom, not noticing the door. The door swung back and forth before colliding against her head. She stood there and took the blow. He stood there and watched—out of confusion, he would later tell himself. Annabel did not make a sound, did not seem to register the pain. Then she fell against him. There was nothing holding her up but him.

"Knock-knock?"

She leaned her head back and squinted. "Daddy."

"It's me. Gēge."

"I want Daddy. Daddy." She nestled her face in his stomach.

Because Annabel refused to stand on her own, he picked her up. He hadn't held her like that for years, not since she'd mastered her legs. Once she turned five, she permitted only Daddy to carry her, dragging her feet on the ground when his mother gave it a try. His father would scoop her up with one arm, as effortless as ladling soup. *I want Daddy.* Annabel was small for her age and Jack had been doing push-ups every night in preparation for Coach Becker's class, but his arms still shook with her weight as he climbed the stairs.

In Annabel's room, his parents were pancaked against each other. His mother had a hand draped over his father's chest, and her face pressed against his. She looked as if she were sniffing up the loose wax from his ear. Surely, she'd rolled into him in her sleep. Jack's arms gave out, and his sister tumbled onto an open space on the bed—the landing not as graceful as he'd hoped—and his mother's head bobbed. Her callused foot peeked out from the comforter and twitched.

Jack stood by the bed. It felt right to stay there, to be the one to watch over the sleeping. To witness his parents closer to each other now than he could remember seeing them while they were awake. His sister kept fidgeting. His mother, still asleep, untangled from his father and maneuvered the girl over her own body to the center of the bed. No one woke; Jack was the one person who could see. There was a thrill to keeping it all to himself, like holding photographs of his family taken by a private detective.

His father was remarkably still. Back when he'd yelled out at night, he was simply having the *wrong dreams*, Jack's mother had told him. Then Annabel was born and they moved, and his father seemed to have only the right dreams. Maybe one day he'd forget that his father had ever had trouble sleeping.

Annabel's nightlights—five of them, in the shape of safari animals—dragged shadows across the ceiling. Jack was still gazing at them when his father's voice croaked out below him. In the middle of the night in a suburb like Plano, sounds pass one by one. A car engine idles across the street. The house's air-conditioning kicks in. The sheer curtains, brilliant with car light, rustle in response. A car door cracks open.

"You. Where are you?"

Jack moved closer. "I'm here."

His father had not turned his head. He could have been talking to the ceiling. "Where?"

Jack waved a hand. "Here."

"Érzi." His father saw him now. "Water?"

Jack took the empty glass from the nightstand and refilled it from the tap in the adjoining bathroom. When he returned to the bed, his father was sitting up against the headboard the way one might after a long nap. He looked as if he'd woken up in that position and was trying to figure out how he'd gotten there. When Jack presented him with the glass, he hesitated.

"You asked for water, so."

"Yes, yes. Thank you." His father gulped it down.

After his father finished the glass, Jack took it without prompting. He refilled it and returned it to him, who nodded and finished it again.

He had never attended to his father like this, and certainly not in the middle of the night, but it was easier than having to answer for why he'd been in the room, watching them sleeping. For once, he was grateful that his father didn't ask. He fetched yet another glass.

After the third glass, his father said, "I know it is late." He did not tell Jack to go. Maybe he was saying it out of appreciation, Jack thought. *I know it is late, yet you are here, watching over us.*

"More water?" Jack asked.

His father declined with a wave of his hand. He rolled his head around his neck, muttering something about having the strangest dream, though he could not remember it. He could remember only the strangeness. Was Jack here, he said, to bring him back down to earth? He said it as if Jack's presence was not strange at all.

It felt good to be seen as useful, thought Jack. You have to walk through a place as if you've known it all your life. Like his first American teacher, an Oklahoman married to a man she met backpacking in Finland, who'd taken his second-grade class one day past a field of tall grass to a small pond near Logan Elementary School. It was only a few acres, but surrounded by the biggest trees he'd seen in Plano, the parkways and walled neighborhoods out of sight, it looked wild. Mrs. Karjalainen did not teach them about the blackland prairie, the buffalo and wildfires. She did not talk about the people who'd crossed through first. She claimed beavers were around, and though he never saw any, Jack had thought her worldly enough to believe her.

He'd brought his father to the pond one afternoon, not too long after the class, pretending he'd discovered it on his own. He pointed to heaps of brushwood and called them beaver dams. Jack had been in America for less than a year then, and his father had seemed impressed by his quick grasp of the land. He suggested to Jack that they lure out the beavers. He fashioned a beaver pole out of a stick, gathered leaf stems and vines, tied a horse apple at the end for bait. Neither of them had even gone fishing before. Jack knew that their venture wouldn't amount to much, but it was nice sitting on the fallen leaves and hearing the creek murmuring.

Looking at his father in bed now, Jack wanted to ask him if he remembered that day at the pond the way Jack did. Could they have spent an entire afternoon there, searching for beavers? Had his father scooped up mud with his hands, just to point out wisps of what he claimed was beaver hair? His father had said then how he could live by the water, that it reminded him of China. His China was so different from Jack's China, but the pond, that was the same. This room now, the same.

Jack was about to bring up the pond, and the sounds, and the beavers, when a cry erupted from the other side of the bed. Annabel. He had almost forgotten about Annabel.

Her cries were loud enough to finally wake his mother. Jack slipped away before she noticed him. Down the hallway, the cries somehow grew louder. Stop, his mother said. There was fussing, groaning. *Stop*, his mother said, each time in the same even tone. *Stop . . . stop* . . . Annabel would wake up the next morning with a lump on her forehead and his mother would claim responsibility for it—a crime, she assumed, committed in her sleep. His father would joke that his mother would need to bubble-wrap her elbows from now on. Jack would not mention the swinging kitchen door, or their middle-of-the-night conversation, because what was there to say? *Daddy*, he heard before he closed his bedroom door. *Daddy*.

• • •

"Daddy," a sleepwalking Annabel said when Jack found her outside this November night. "Daddy," she said, as he steered her away from the cricket-dappled streetlight, the sewage creek, the dark and dangerous roads. "Daddy," as if she were willing Jack to be stronger, someone who wasn't her brother. They were going back to Daddy, that big shapeless mound under the covers, a refuge Jack could never be. The wind chimes had gone quiet and the only sounds outside were the ones he and his sister made. He walked on the side closest to the road, nudging her slippers' back when they veered. A paper Starbucks cup, left upright on the sidewalk, tilted over before they reached it. There was no breeze, no motive for a cup to fall. It was still too warm for the bushes to shiver—and neither, Jack decided, would he.

"Daddy. Daddydaddydaddy." Annabel wouldn't stop. They turned onto Plimpton Court. Before she could say another word, Jack reached for her. His hand became bigger, clutching hers. He did not realize how hard he was squeezing. He was back to being the boy who'd woken up by himself in America. That was how he recalled the journey: he was in the plane, face down with the āyí's hand on his back, and then he wasn't. He'd assumed it was morning, except the room was impossibly dark. The mattress beneath him caved in so deep it felt broken. There was murmuring outside. Only when he planted his feet on the ground did he know he could stand. Outside the room, another mattress leaned against the wall beside his suitcase. He walked down the hallway, ready for a fight. He didn't have his sword anymore, but he had his fists. He had only himself to protect.

At the end of the hallway, he met his parents. His mother no longer looked like the woman in the photograph. She sat down by a spread of cold dumplings, her back strained against a chair. His father placed a hand on her belly, rubbing where it swelled. His hand looked heavy, his touch light. He spoke to the belly with words that didn't sound like English or Mandarin, or any recognizable dialect. By the time either of them noticed Jack—his mother, first—he'd lowered his fists. Jack took in the tight knots of her smile.

Behind her, stacked against the wall like a second wall, were tiny pajamas, shoes, hats. Mittens, jackets, blankets, bibs, little square cloths. A car seat and rocking chair and stroller filled with summer clothes, winter clothes, day clothes, night clothes. Sheets and covers and comforters and sacks. Shampoos and soaps. Ointments spilling out of a medicine kit. Stuffed animals, dolls, rattles, a cartoon airplane, a mini piano still in packing, with words he could recognize: *Try me!*

Diapers. So many diapers. A castle of diapers. Jack must have been looking at the diapers when his father noticed him, taking his eyes, for the first time, away from the belly.

On Plimpton Court, Annabel shook loose from his hand and marched on. When Jack blocked her path, she crashed into his chest. Every time he got in front of her, trying to slow her, she sleepwalked into him. They bumped into each other all the way down the sidewalk, house by house by house. That was when he realized the front door to their house was open.

From the other side, the door became unrecognizable. Plano was not like the places in his books, where doors creaked open after midnight. He had never seen such a thing. Standing on the cobbled pathway, he could not reconcile the door that he'd forgotten to close with the door he faced now: a framed black rectangle, a portal into a darker darkness.

"Annabel," he whispered, but his sister could not hear.

If only they could stay like this: Annabel strutting toward the open door, in the middle of kicking back the welcome mat. Loose dust stickered in the air. Across the street, a sprinkler head rising out of the earth. If only the two of them could look back at the path they'd taken, from that time he'd found her curled around the toilet to this strange door, a path paved by histories they would never know because they could not look back. If only they could look forward and know what was coming. Maybe their mother, finally returning from work. Or their father, waiting for them in the dark. If only Jack could tell his parents that he had led Annabel away from unthinkable dangers. An assassin who masqueraded during daytime as the family dentist. A birthday party magician who spent his off-hours making children disappear. A terrorist who lived not across the ocean but in their neighborhood, who looked like any other person, a person who was angry about something. If only Jack could do something, be something, protect his sister from something, in this place where nothing happened.

"Nervous?" his mother had asked from the hospital bed, the night Annabel had first needed protecting. Three months he had been in America. Three months he'd ruled over an empty apartment while his mother tinkered with microchips and his father drove around North Texas photographing strangers. Three months he'd learned English by reading the backs of TV dinners and repeating lines from the American version of the *Power Rangers*. Three months he'd opened doors he shouldn't have for Bible and textbook salespeople, introducing himself not as Chéng Xiǎo Jiàn but as Jack. It had been only three months.

"Hands out," his father said. He turned to Jack with the bundle.

"Sit down, kěbù kěyǐ," his mother said.

"Careful with her head," his father said.

"Xiǎoxīn," his mother said. "Support her head."

"*Gentle* with her head," his father said. "Qīngqīng diǎn'r."

"Use your other hand, too," his mother said.

"Bring her into your arms," his father said.

"Relax your shoulders," his mother said.

"Lower now," his father said, "slowly, mànmàn diǎn'r."

Annabel was swaddled so snugly that Jack couldn't feel her breathing. Her eyes appeared halfway closed, as if she'd lost control of the muscles to shut them all the way. He pressed a hand, as lightly as he could, to her chest. He couldn't feel the pitter-patter of a life.

Jack considered the possibility that the girl had died. That upon his touch, she had gone cold and stiff. A consideration, outlandish as it was, that made his arms weak. His knees buckled with the weight of the soft mass. He was holding a corpse. Jack would remember this differently—would even remember it in English—but the truth was he'd just urinated. It was less than a stream and more than a trickle. His thighs were damp and his pants began to darken. He tried to pass this off as sweat. The piss smell and the new baby smell combined into a kind of sweat smell. Some of his piss had probably gotten on Annabel's blanket.

Then the girl in his arms yawned. His sister's mouth went

crooked, her nose rose, and her eyebrows canted toward the middle. It was as if through the yawn, she had swallowed all of the sound in the world. Gone were the gleeful whispers from his mother to his father. His father kissing his mother between the eyes. The stops he made down her nose to the fuzz above her lips. His mother giggling, telling his father to quit it. Then the lens of a camcorder sliding open, its click and hum. There was only his sister's yawn.

Annabel stirred, wriggling in her blanket. Jack brought the crook of his arm under her head and swayed her left and right. A good sway to nudge her back to sleep. It was a challenge finding the right rhythm. *One and . . . two and . . . three and . . .*

"Easy," their father said, and from behind the camera he touched Jack's arm.

2

Plano was a suburb of oven mitts and motion sensors. Voice recognition and outlet plug covers. Automatic sliding doors, timed fluorescent lights, sleep mode, speakerphone. Intercoms and cameras in offices, and sometimes in homes. Sprinkler systems and car washes. Air hand dryers. In the Shops at Legacy's dimly lit restaurants, a bathroom attendant. Whether Patty Cheng received her fajitas at On the Border or Kitchen by Javier, the server would warn, as if to translate the sizzling sound, "Hot—hot!" She could point to any necklace under a glass case, and a jeweler with perpetually moisturized hands would fetch it. Flip-flops never went out of season. Patty always wore shoes, slippers in the house. Her neighbors, the Crawfords, set their central air-conditioning to seventy degrees and didn't lay their hands on the thermostat until Thanksgiving. The weather could be hot, cold, or just unpleasant enough to serve as the subject of small talk, but still Patty hopped from home garage to office garage and back without stepping outside for days. Toll tag pasted to her dashboard, she made the thirty-seven-minute trip downtown in the gray light of dawn without rolling down the window.

On the highway before morning rush hour, Patty towered above the Super Walmarts and Hobby Lobbys and their empty parking lots. She switched lanes without using her blinker and rode the HOV lane solo. The eight-person Chevy Tahoe lifted her like a palanquin—not as high as the other Plano parents' Hummers, but still she could spot the dust and bird droppings on the roof of a passing sedan. This felt like an accomplishment. In the gridlocks of Tianjin, she'd never imagined driving at all, let alone this fast and high. On the highway, no taxis, bicycles, rickshaws, mopeds, or bodies interrupted her. Machines romped across earthwork and concrete, programmed with two rules: always move forward, and do not, under any circumstances, touch each other.

On maps, the northern suburbs, veined by highways, also did not appear to touch. Plano and Allen sprawled out east of Tollway, Carrollton, and open fields and megachurches to the west. Frisco, where houses were cheaper and schools marginally less competitive, sat atop 121. South of George Bush,

Richardson buzzed with its Chinatown and growing hub of tech companies, and farther east, Garland paraded its lakes and fancy hotels. South of Tollway and past 635, one could glimpse the mansions of Highland Park. Out of view, farther west, lay the Arlington of Dallas Cowboys and Texas Rangers fame, and beyond that Fort Worth, the *FW* in *DFW*. In Patty's mind, the *D* consisted only of entrances and exits.

In the weeks before she started at Texas Semiconductor, she and Liang had explored downtown Dallas, turning over fruit at the farmers market, posing in front of the dandelion tower, pretending to be cowboys among the cattle sculptures. Taking a wrong exit on the way home one day, they'd threaded through a landfill and one-way streets: chain-link fences, screen doors, car bodies parked on cinder blocks on overgrown lawns devoid of trees, houses as small as the one she imagined Liang had grown up in. At least in China, though, the countryside contained formation and vegetation, disarray that felt natural even when it wasn't. America's landscapes, on the other hand, were not hers to fret about, so Patty told Liang that the flashing tank on the dashboard meant that their ten-year-old Volvo had twenty more miles to go, that they didn't have to step foot on streets with no sidewalks, or ask for directions at the liquor store by the tents under I-45. They could find any highway among the clot of them, aim north, and before the end of a radio interview, traffic permitting, be back in Plano.

Of course, in a metroplex with almost no public transportation, traffic was not always permitting, especially in afternoon rush hour. Often, driving home from work, Patty would get lost or stuck or both. She missed detours and temporary bridges, the highways in an eternal state of construction. Today, weaving through an uncompleted five-level interchange, she found herself in a traffic jam one hundred and twenty feet in the sky. In the early evening sun, the Tahoe was redolent of expired air freshener trees.

On the radio, a traffic reporter was saying something about roadblocks and massive delays. "Clus-ter-fuck," Patty said aloud. It was her coworkers' term of choice for the daily conference call where everyone, Indian and American, spoke at once. *Hello, Raj*, she'd said thousands of times by now. *Yes, I hear you, Karl. Chethan, hello. Okay, hey Pranav. How are you today, gentlemen? Nice weather over there? By the way, this is Patty.* It was protocol to say your name after connecting to the Texas Semi long-distance bridge, but as the lead States-based designer assigned to a development team in Bangalore, she set up the calls. *You sound . . . slow this morning, Karl. Too much toddy last night? You say what? Already six in the evening? Maybe I am the one drinking.*

A giddiness came over her as a man in a Lexus tried and failed to pass her. Reaching another standstill, she shifted to park so that she could scratch an itch under her foot. *No, Brent cannot join us this morning*, she remembered saying that morning. *I mean evening. A busy man, Mr. MBA*. Her boss, five years younger than she, had skipped the November check-in. As if to assert her own authority, Patty had held the others on the call longer than scheduled: *Well, gentlemen, since it's so late already . . . a little later is no problem, right?* Always Raj, Karl, Chethan, and Pranav told her *No problem, I will handle*, even when there was a problem, something they couldn't handle, so perhaps with their mics muted they'd proceeded to call her a tyrant, a bitch. They were engineers, not customer service, and Patty was no better than those Americans who called Amazon to complain about the paper cuts they got reading their books, hungry to unload their indignation on the accent on the other line, before demanding to speak to a manager. No, Chethan would have railed to Pranav, he'd gone to the Indian Institute of Science and was not a brain for loan, and not to mention, Pranav would have added, they all had families waiting for them at home. It wasn't their fault if she didn't.

The voices on the radio were getting louder, as if to speak over Patty's musings. Nineteen Italians killed in Iraq were laid to rest. Three days after PFC Jessica Lynch's book deal, someone had threatened to leak nude photographs of her. Listeners trickled in with their thoughts, live. "We can't just let this happen!" one gravelly voice said, the way football coaches in movies give speeches. "We still have to buy that goddamn book!"

"God . . . damn," Patty said, as the producers cut off the coach's voice.

She was pretty sure Mr. MBA Brent knew she had a family. When he'd passed her on his way out, an hour ago, he'd teasingly ordered her to go home. Darrell, the cleaning guy, certainly did—evenings when he found her still at work, he'd remind her with aggressive good cheer that her kids were hungry, and maybe he needed to have a talk with the boss man on her behalf. Was it possible that her team in Bangalore did *not* know she had a family? Soon after they'd begun working together in July, she remembered, she had told them about leaving Tianjin at twenty-four. But had she mentioned whom she'd left behind? They knew about the master's from the University of Houston, but not the PhD she'd lost after funding dried up and she was forced to apply for industry jobs in order to ensure Jack would get his visa. Did she tell them that as a student she'd helped develop a method for transferring electric energy from a power source to an electric load through nothing but an electromagnetic field? She'd powered a 40-watt lightbulb from a meter away, *without a wire.* If she got them on the phone right now, would they care to hear about that?

She pictured them now, on the other side of the world. Brilliant men kissing their wives and sons and daughters goodbye, the taste of dosa and filtered kaapi still on their lips as they rushed to catch the company shuttle before morning gridlock. They would be making their way to fancy tech parks, with perfectly proportioned lakes and honeycombed offices, while Patty was the one crawling back to her family, mile after congested mile. All those nights, while she nodded off during Annabel's one hundred kisses, Raj and Karl and Chethan and Pranav would have been leaning back in their ergonomic chairs, their leather shoes propped up on the table next to a computer screen filling up with algorithms and 32-bit numbers, preparing themselves for the conference call they were going to have with her after she woke up. While Annabel clamped her teeth on Patty's lips and refused to let go, they would be in their office cafeteria biting down on the thigh of a freshly roasted chicken and laughing about the fart the office administrator had let out down the hall before she'd made it to the bathroom. The next day Patty would snap awake. Four thirty a.m. No alarms, just reflex, seconds to reboot. A mumbling Liang and ragged-breathed Annabel turning onto their sides, reaching across the space she'd vacated. She'd be the first to nose out of the garage, and in her cubicle under the commercial ceiling tiles and timed fluorescent lights that had not yet activated, would connect to Texas Semi's long-distance bridge a couple hours before her Bangalore team would leave for the day.

In Patty's car, the phone was ringing. She picked up without looking at the screen.

"This is Patty," she said.

"I know. I called you," said a voice in Mandarin.

"Oh. I thought. Never mind."

"It's six fifteen," Liang said.

The clock on the dashboard read 6:22 p.m., but there was no need to correct Liang. Over the phone, her husband sounded like someone from the past. A recording.

"Did you receive my email?"

"Mm-hmm. You are not waiting to eat, right? The traffic. There was an accident—"

"An accident."

She had turned down the radio to a murmur by then. The air in the car tasted metallic. Had there been an accident, or had she imagined the radio saying that? "Six-car pileup, I heard. I should reach it soon. The ambulance is stuck behind me somewhere."

"Annabel asked me today why you're never here in the morning," Liang said. "She dreams you never come back from India."

"India. What can she know about India?"

"Don't you understand? She believes that every night, after she falls asleep, you fly away to India. And we ask ourselves why she won't sleep alone."

She wanted to remind Liang that their efforts to get their daughter to sleep alone had been halfhearted at best. The three of them had simply moved from sleeping together on their bed downstairs to squeezing onto Annabel's bed upstairs. Was it Annabel who was making them stick to her? One day, she wanted to remind Liang, their daughter would be fine sleeping on her own. Would they?

Liang persisted: "Should I tell her Māma is going to be home late from India, too?"

Tell her Māma is late for a reason, Patty could say. She had finally graduated from peripheral I/O templates to something bigger. No, it was not a revolutionary study into the wireless transmission of electricity, but she and her team were teaching a digital signal processor, or DSP, to convert elaborate mathematical calculations into basic operations, translating algorithms faster than before in order to power Motorola's newest, sleekest flip phone. As the system architect, it was up to Māma to corral them multiple times a week for clusterfucks, so that they could work out how to design an engine that, beyond processing information, communicated like a brain, one that sent messages to data memory and I/O ports and the outside world, realizing a fully functioning body. One day she would tell Annabel all of that.

"Tell me, Qīng-Qīng." Liang took a long breath. "Are you still at work?"

"I told you, the traffic—"

"The traffic."

Accident. Traffic. Words Liang repeated as if they meant

something entirely different to him. And maybe they did. He was no longer the man who, upon a chance assignment from a client, lugged lenses and tripods and reflectors from Tianjin to Beijing to photograph a dying woman who'd put on makeup she couldn't afford so her husband could properly grieve her image when she was gone. No longer the man who drove their Volvo beyond the urban knots of Texas to places where he was the sole Chinese person anyone had ever seen, so he could get paid in cash to photograph backyard weddings and fifty-person homecomings. His windowless studio was ten minutes from their house in Plano. He was more building manager than photographer these days, with most of the business, as Patty had predicted, coming from high school girls who rented the rooms after school, posing with the wedding-photo-booth-style props and taking their own pictures with the remote-controlled cameras. At first Liang had resisted her suggestions to rebrand, but after she'd taken him through the wringer of private school and college planning seminars and dangled the threat of quitting her job so she could properly raise Annabel, he'd relented. Before long he was doubling down on his new role, using the money they were supposed to save to hire assistants for weekday shifts, only going in some weekends for the rare assignment. *More time for the children*, he'd reasoned, borrowing the words Patty had once used to convince him.

"Where is this traffic?" he said now, over the phone.

Hǔfù hǔzǐ, so why couldn't Liang be more like Jack? Their jīn gǒu would ask her with genuine interest where or why she was going, where or how she had been, and when she would smile or sigh and say, "Work," her avid young watcher of CNN would release her from his stare, as if the word weighed enough, as if he could hold all of *work* or *debt* or *mass destruction* in his palm. She spoke to her son with words that felt big, meant little. In spite of this, he did not ask her for more. He did not ask, Patty wanted to believe, because he understood his mother—understood, somehow, that she could hold only so much. Even a spoon felt heavy, coming home from another day that proved both utterly predictable and out of her control. Their years apart had made the boy profound, enough so that he offered the generosity of his caution. He did not press her the way his father did, did not demand explanation or assurance. Did not ask her in the morning what she'd been dreaming about, as if he expected her to say, "Well, *you*."

Better not to dream, she wanted to tell Liang sometimes. *You should know this better than anyone.* But Liang's sleep troubles were finally a thing of the past, and they had not talked about them for years. In Plano, they talked about *growth opportunities*. About the DSP, for instance, that one-inch-by-one-inch microchip that unlocked user speeds never before possible. Promotions, cubicles with doors, offices with windows, corner offices with windows. A guest room, a mortgage, a new SUV, a lawyer to recover the lost green card application that had made it too risky to fly back to China even for a visit, to hold her parents' and brothers' hands once more. The DSP was the future. It gave her a reason not to look back.

Somewhere ahead on 75, an ambulance wailed. A real one, this time. Patty strained to hear it over the honking, the memories, over Liang's voice on the phone, *Qīng-Qīng. The email . . .*

Honking.

Honking, behind her.

"Cars are moving now, have to go," she said, and hung up before Liang could say more about the email. She straightened up in her seat, nudged the Tahoe forward, filling in less than ten feet of concrete. Behind her, the man in the Lexus braked, hard. She watched in the rearview mirror as he punched the steering wheel and slapped the dashboard. Maybe Liang was doing something similar now, with the phone that sat on the kitchen counter.

"What do I do?" she said aloud, imagining bringing the problem to her Bangalore team. *What do I do about my family?*

Who? they would ask. And she would ask herself the same question. Who were these people she lived with, and what did they do when she was not there? Perhaps Annabel was hopping from chair to chair around the kitchen table, knocking over chopsticks and bowls, using Māma's absence as an excuse not to eat her bok choy and mushrooms. Jack, on the other hand, would be racing to finish his food, always pitted against a competitor who wasn't there, his head hanging over his bowl, a head too large for his neck, a boy whose body had grown into solidity before proportionality. And Liang: he would be staring outside, as if a clock were pinned to the sky. His wife was not only late, but late again.

It was Patty who had emailed Liang first, earlier in the afternoon, to tell him that she might be late. She'd remembered he was going to play poker with his friends in the evening, and reassured him that she would be back in time for him to go. They didn't need to wait on her for dinner. They didn't need to worry about her at all.

He'd emailed back, almost immediately:

> I wonder I should forget poker. I mean: I wonder I
> should not go. Maybe you don't want me go? I
> don't know, I mean, how you feel every time I go. I
> see the real you when I come back. Like I did
> something wrong, like my smiling and good time
> made you have bad time. I mean: I wonder it
> would be better for you I stay home.
>
> I feel I have not seen you for so long, even we
> live in same house, share same bed. Sometime, I
> wake up, don't remember where you are. I know

Annabel's bed is small. But I think Qing-Qing—
maybe problem is, Annabel is problem. I mean:
problem is we sharing ourselves with her. At her
age Annabel should sleep in her own bed, yes, but
also by herself—this is what teachers say. Maybe
tonight, we sleep downstairs, just us.

I know you have long day. So maybe you wish
you have our nice big bed downstairs, for yourself.
I mean: maybe you wish I am not there. But . . .
maybe not. Maybe you wish you can be with me,
just me, so we can sleep like we sleep before,
remember? With our back turn to each other, your
foot touch my foot, like you want to make sure
I am there. I mean: I want to sleep like this, with
you. Knowing you are there. Even I wake up and
you are gone, knowing: you are there.

What do you think? Drive safe.

Best Regards,
Liang Cheng
YOUR Home Studios
"Fun Self-Portraits, One Click Away!"

It was the longest email she could remember Liang sending
her in years, stumbling in both directions as if he could not

pause to think through the words, could not press backspace, as if they were back in Tianjin, and he were penning one of the frantic letters he'd sent her days after he'd taken pictures of her graduating class on the front steps of the Nankai University administrative building. He was Chéng Liàng then, the fidgety and handsome photographer her school had hired. Patty had walked up to him after the session, because she hadn't liked the way he'd rushed through it. She suspected her eyes were closed for most of the shots.

How little he must think of their graduation, she said to him. Did he think they'd accomplished nothing? Earlier she'd noticed Liang's strong build, the sturdy air about him, but once she got going he looked upon her with fear, as if it were she who'd hired him. He did not protest when she went back with him to his studio, nearly an hour away from the university, a run-down former accounting office with one room converted into a darkroom. He shared it with three other men, all of whom had gone home by the time she and Liang arrived. She realized, as Liang began hanging up the developing photographs, that for him this *was* home. Off to the side of his makeshift office was a daybed, no bigger than the folding cot tucked away in her parents' closet. The studio smelled like sweat. She took a cigarette from Liang and he did not say anything when she fumbled with the lighter.

It was her first cigarette. She had a second, a third, a fourth.

They talked about her studies. Her high marks. Her less successful brothers. How the eldest had taken the two-hour bus to Tiananmen two summers ago, in order to sit among the protestors. How he came home before the blood began to flow, relaying tales of students driven to hunger strikes, of pop stars from Taiwan sleeping in the tents among the people, of speeches that made the hairs on his already-balding head stand up. She told Liang stories that were really her brother's stories because she had not been there, had opted to be a student who went to school, who paved a future for herself by memorizing the equations that governed the world, not by sitting on baked concrete and bickering with other students about which songs to sing for the cameras. She went on talking in Liang's studio, learning nothing about him except that he nodded and agreed and made the way she saw the world seem less ridiculous.

She realized, after they began kissing, that she was going to miss the last bus. *My parents will think I am dead.* The thought gave her a little thrill, until she remembered that the man she was now straddling was someone who could make that true. What did she know? Liang could have been anyone.

She tried to lift the hem of his shirt. He patted her hand away. He let her kiss him some more, but did not offer more. Would a killer be so shy? Would a killer be hesitant to be touched? All her life she had trusted, above all, herself. That night she took the lead, and though their clothes did not come off, she told him when to kiss her, where to touch her, until they fell asleep and she could not tell him what to do any longer. When he later woke in a sweat, his hands thrashing the air above them, she trusted that this new feeling that now seized her was not fear but concern, a desperate concern that was a close cousin to love. Here was a person who needed help, and here she was, helping him. She held down Liang's arms as best she could, held them as he swatted and even swung at her, though he missed. *Chéng Liàng*, she called to him. *Chéng Liàng*, the way her mother would state her brothers' names when she was angry. *Chéng. Liàng.* Perhaps it was in that naming that he recognized himself, and who was calling him— and he stopped.

The next morning, Liang could not recall what had happened, but he piled on apology after apology. In his letters, in the spaces between more apologies and appreciations, he professed his love to her—how indebted he was to her, how humbled before her, how he would do whatever it took to make her time with him more comfortable. At no point did he say *It will never happen again*, and she was grateful for that honesty. Among the nights to follow there would be, on occasion, another sleepless one. Sometimes, Liang would keep waking up; other times, he'd groan or even shout. She wondered if he had ever slept with another person before her. At night, she became his harness and his witness, the one to tell him what had happened, and who he had been when it happened. The initial thrill of keeping the nights a secret from her parents faded. In its place, a mission, one not unlike the studies on electrical currents she hoped to conduct in graduate school: she wanted to know the unknowable, to know it so intimately she could not only tend to it but master it.

Now here she was, stuck in traffic and avoiding Liang's emails. Patty had wished desperately to share his response with anyone in the cubicles around her. She'd imagined copying and pasting the last section and sending it to her Bangalore team with the subject line, "Thoughts, gentlemen?" But people were already filing home, one by one, two by two, until it was only her and Darrell the cleaning guy, reminding her of the time.

There was one thing Patty liked about driving, and it was why she did not mind going to work early, or even driving into traffic on the way home. She could be away from her email. The car was a space where she could be free of the work she'd left and the work that awaited her. Because it was work, to decipher who her husband was, and what he wanted.

She looked in the rearview mirror. "Thoughts, gentlemen?" she said aloud.

But she could not imagine an answer to the question.

. . .

For the next hour, she floated along with the crowd, watching the sun come down. The man in the Lexus behind her massaged his head. Rooms in the surrounding hotels came to life and business travelers pulled back their curtains. Maybe traffic in Dallas looked beautiful from up there, Patty thought. A gold bracelet of lights, turned ever so slightly around the wrist. The wave of cars crawled past the invisible lines of subdivisions, municipalities, cities, counties, electoral districts she didn't know could be redrawn or why.

At 7:35, traffic began to thin.

There seemed no reason for it. Five lanes had contracted into four, yet the pace was picking up. The ambulance had passed, but there was no indication of an accident anywhere. When she turned the radio back up, it had moved on to stock market chatter.

The expanse of concrete in front of her skipped to the length of ten cars, twenty cars. For a few seconds Patty tensed. Perhaps it was a trick of the changing light, but the freedom ahead seemed untenable, even dangerous. Compared to this, traffic was a cozy hotel robe. She reluctantly pressed the accelerator. The car lumbered forward. She pressed a little harder, and the world jumped closer.

She took the next exit, though it wasn't the correct one.

Driving slowly, she finally checked her phone. Three missed calls from Home. The beam of blue shot out from the screen and into her mouth, and she had a sudden desire to swallow the phone. Instead, she shoved the DSP-powered device into her purse and made a right on Plano Parkway. Her fingers stiffened on the wheel, as if to send warnings to her mind. Too early! Wrong way! After she crossed two intersections, both with NO U-TURN signs, she thought she might as well keep on.

Patty should have turned back when she reached St. John's, the private boys' school she and Liang were failing to save up enough money to send Jack to. Or at the Taiwanese café where Annabel had once choked on tapioca balls. At the intersection where a high school boy, racing his friends during lunch break, had crashed into a stoplight, she should have gone back. It had been two years since the accident and the boy's friends and family had stopped leaving flowers at the corner, but suddenly it came to her that this was where a portion of a seventeen-year-old's skull had exited a windshield. She drove on. Twenty minutes later she made a right into the apartment complex where she and Liang had first lived in Plano.

It was too dark to make out the numbers on each building, but she felt her way around by memory. The copper-tinted mailboxes where she'd waited for her USCIS notices. The handicap ramp where lanky white skateboarders shot trick videos. She pulled up at a parking space next to two locked dumpsters, the spot that used to be hers. She turned off the engine, and all the voices, the ones on the radio and Raj and Karl and Chethan and Pranav, went quiet. Then it was too quiet. She flipped on the hazard signal. There was no hazard, but a sound would help her to stay awake.

On her phone: four missed calls from Home. When had the fourth come in? Her thumb hovered over the grimy keypad while her eyes skipped from window to window of the building before her: glimpses of TV antennas, the drooping petals of houseplants. She could not remember which apartment had been theirs. The not knowing saddened her, and she felt an urge to corroborate with Liang.

Before she could change her mind, she was calling Home back. Even with the phone a good distance from her ear, she could hear the ringing. A woman in her underwear walked up to one of the second-floor windows. The blinds were suspended halfway, so Patty could see only the lower half of her body. The woman's underwear was a simple beige like most of Patty's, loose around the hips. The woman's legs were strong and limber, like a gymnast's.

"Greetings," said a familiar voice. "You have reached the Chengs. We are not here to answer your call, so please feel free to leave a message and we will feel free to answer your call upon our return. Thank you."

When they first arrived at this apartment, Liang had spent

an afternoon crafting that message, and they had been able to keep both number and message when they moved. Patty had heard it so often she could recite it in her sleep, yet now, as she watched the stranger pace around her living room, the rise and fall of Liang's recorded voice sounded too loud, too self-conscious. There was a formality to the opening and ending, something forced in the way he presented them as *the Chengs*. Yes, it was still strange to hear the way he pronounced it, the *Cheng* almost rhyming with *pain*. But she had learned to say it this way, too. Patty's legal last name was still Hong, but it wasn't being lumped in as a Cheng that she minded, either. It was the way Liang emphasized the packlike nature of the word, almost hissing the *s* at the end. The desperation in it, the sinking his claws into it.

Not to mention that, at the time of the recording, there had been only the two of them. The Chengs! When had they become not Patty and Liang but *the Chengs*? The easy answer, she supposed, was when they got married. It had been a fairly straight line from spending nights in his studio to discussing their marriage with her parents (Liang didn't have parents with whom to discuss). After they got married, the discussions dissipated, even as her questions sharpened. Why did he lavish her with kisses, but shy away from sex? Why did he eagerly share stories he'd heard as a child, but not stories about *being* a child, and the people who'd taken care of him? Then there were the restless nights: how long would they go on? He scoffed at the idea of seeing a doctor, and Patty wondered if he was embarrassed, as if, like an adult who had never learned how to walk or chew solid food, he had simply failed to learn how to sleep. Their last year in Tianjin, he parried her questions with more questions: Why did they have to live with her parents? Why continue her PhD applications while pregnant? He did not want her going on her solitary walks along the Hai River. Did not want her away at all. His power came from more than his sinewy hands: it came from needing her, always.

"Message ended."

Patty looked at the phone in her lap. She thought she had hung up, but instead she'd left the longest message allowed. Now her breathing was stored in the answering machine at her kitchen counter, and that gave her a stab of queasiness. She dug her nails into the steering wheel. In the apartment in front of her, the woman's legs kept moving out of view and back. Was she cleaning? Working out? Maybe she was like Patty: thinking. Even with half the window veiled, it was clear the woman had the room to herself. Watching her in her underwear was oddly calming. To be alone, maybe that was all Patty wanted. Only if that were true, why did she always go back in the direction of people? Why did she create *more* people? Maybe she wanted to suffer, she thought. Maybe she was still being conditioned by the very propaganda that the students in Tiananmen had sacrificed their bodies to fight against. Or maybe what she wanted was to be alone, and not alone. To have the power to be both.

There had been a time when such a thing had seemed possible. She had received her fellowship for the University of Houston, and Liang had somberly agreed to stay in Tianjin with their son, at least through the end of her coursework, so she could get her bearings and they could save money. A temporary arrangement, she'd assured him. She would make America a home for them. But as soon as Patty arrived in Houston, Liang begged her to apply for his F-2 visa. They would build this home together, he said. As for Jack, the boy already spent days and nights with his grandparents, and it was not a stretch to extend the arrangement. Liang would join Patty. Money would be tight but they would make America a home— a home for Jack. Liang spoke with the urgency of his early letters, with a desire to woo her, and she was not sure if she had done a good enough job hiding her disappointment, even as she acquiesced.

The Chengs. Maybe that was when it began: when Liang followed her to Houston six months after she got there. And yet, she remembered their early years together with fondness— the disappointment giving way to relief, to have someone from the past with whom to wade through the future, to untangle the webs of a new country. They acquired a more mature kind of love for each other, a camaraderie bolstered by the many hours every day they spent apart, her on campus, him at his odd assignments. There were fewer hours in America, or at least it felt that way. When they came home to their tiny student apartment, they brought little pieces from their private worlds into the home they shared, which helped them see that home anew. She felt in their partnership a momentum again, and she trusted it, and in that trust came a longing for more—for Jack—that kept her awake deep into the nights when Liang was sleeping soundly.

Then the next disappointment: her funding was going to be cut—and then it was all gone. The pain of the news carved a space in her gut that would never be dissolved, but the relief that rose out of it sent her hurtling forward. She could transfer her credits to graduate early with a master's and take a job, and bring Jack to America earlier. When she told Liang, he did not do a good job of hiding his pleasure. Before long, they were moving again. Soon they would be a family of three. That was the happiest summer she could remember.

The summer of moving was also the summer of waiting. Coming back from one of their visits to downtown Dallas, she dashed out of Liang's Volvo and threw up her lunch on the grass by the dumpster. To make matters worse, their neighbor, an elderly woman with a heavy Southern accent, stepped outside to investigate. Earlier that week the woman had told Patty by the mailboxes that Liang was an *oddball*, and Patty had not been sure what she'd meant. Now the neighbor was grinning as she said, *Your husband sure don't know how to drive, but he do know how to make a woman throw up!* before retreating inside.

That night, Patty joined her husband in the shower. In the cramped tub they hadn't yet bought curtains for, they stood so close she saw the little drops on his nose turn into big drops. He shouldn't worry about that old woman, she told him. It wasn't his driving that was making her throw up. As Liang took in her words, the skin around his eyes crinkled. He gave her a puzzled look, shaded with a deep, unrelenting interest, a look that she loved because it encompassed more than who she was—Liang saw who she would be. Then he figured it out, and together they laughed, maybe cried, though it was hard to tell in a shower.

Yes, they had been waiting: not for one child, but two. Patty's parents had warned her about Jack's wildness, but the boy who arrived in America—when he still went by Chéng Xiǎo Jiàn—was not wild but sullen, hǎo tīnghuà. Because they did not have to worry about Jack sticking his finger into electrical outlets or running outside to chase down stray cats, they could leave him to himself. Liang could take assignments from Richardson to Waxahachie, and Patty could leave early in the mornings for work, to make an impression that would last beyond maternity leave—a mother among fathers, unaffected by the children who now saddled her. Even when Liang yelled out at night, Jack did not hound Patty about it. Adults carried a quality he could not yet understand, and Jack seemed okay with that. There had been a streak of wisdom in him even then. At six years old, he knew which questions not to ask.

It was Patty who began to ask the questions. When she watched the way her husband and son maneuvered around each other in the tight hallway, the way during dinner they spoke not so much to each other as through her, she wondered if she had missed an important event in their history. For a school project, Jack had written and illustrated his autobiography, and though he was still learning English, the pages in which his character left his father behind to come to America with his mother—complete with drawings of hamburgers he'd shared with Patty on the plane—had not appeared to be the result of an issue in translation. Perhaps in those six months that Patty had left Liang with Jack in China, something had happened. Perhaps Jack had been wild after all, and that wildness had come from his father. She tried to quiet the voices scraping along the back of her head, asking her why the neighbors were always more at ease talking to her than to Liang. His English was worse than Patty's, but there was something else to their neighbors' hesitance, some reason why they looked only at her, even when she and Liang were together. It had been seven years since Patty had spent that first night at Liang's studio in Tianjin, but only when Jack had joined them in Plano did she begin to see her husband the way others might.

Who was Liang to Jack? Who would Liang be to the new baby? Before Patty could answer these questions, Annabel was born, and they were bringing her home from the hospital. The crib was in their bedroom. As a newborn, Jack had slept in his grandparents' room, something Patty's parents had insisted on, in order to give her and Liang some relief. But in their apartment in Plano, a one-bedroom, Jack had slept on a mattress in the living room, and there was no separate room to put a baby. If Liang had one of his bad nights, how would Annabel respond?

When Patty kissed Liang goodnight and turned away to face the crib, she feared that he knew what was going through her head. That as they lay next to the crib listening to their daughter push through her stuffy nose with the snoring of an old man, Patty worried that one of Liang's flailing arms could land on Annabel's face. When it was just the two of them, such nights had rarely turned—and she hesitated to even use the word—violent. But during her first week at Texas Semiconductor, Patty had to go to the office with a gash on her lip. She'd told her cubicle mates that she'd bumped into the corner of a cabinet. All those new corners in a new home, thankfully her husband had acted quickly and helped patch her up. Which Liang had. He'd helped patch her up.

That first night with Annabel, Patty listened to the baby. She listened to Liang. How hard it was for her husband to do a simple thing, she thought, a thing that came so naturally to a person who'd spent less than a week in life. She was still thinking when he tapped her foot with his. That foot that was always warmer than hers. She told herself then that this was the path they were on, the path she wanted to be on, and she would trust that path, she would keep her foot there, too.

And in a miraculous twist, Liang's sleep troubles vanished after Annabel was born. Patty could not remember him doing more than some harmless tossing and turning when Annabel was in the room. When the four of them moved to Huntington Villa, into their first house, the girl moved into their bed, right between Māma and Daddy—all while her own room lay spick-and-span upstairs, the plastic at first not even leaving the mattress. Upstairs belonged to Jack. No one hundred kisses every night for the boy; one would cause him to say, stretching out the *o* as if the whole word was italicized, *Mom*. He no longer asked Patty if Dad was okay. Perhaps he already knew the answer. She assumed as much, though there were still some days when she would lie awake before dawn, listening to Liang sleeping, and wonder, *Is* he okay? Is he?

In the apartment in front of her, the woman in her underwear had lowered the blinds completely. Lights from a TV screen flashed against them, as in many of the surrounding apartments. In this way, the stranger woman no longer seemed alone. It was as if everyone but Patty was watching the same show. At times the flashes matched up with the ticking of her hazard signal, which she had forgotten she'd left on. On her phone was another missed call. She must have set it to silent mode. She closed her eyes and imagined Liang trying to get their daughter to fall asleep upstairs. Though Annabel was a slow grower, her body, like Liang's, retained its pillowed edges. Their bodies felt intensely good to hug. They could be hugging each other this minute, on that bed. Or, freed of the space that Patty would have taken, they could be stretching out their legs and arms in the most unnatural of positions, not unlike those dead body chalk outlines on *Law & Order*.

The clock on the dashboard read 8:15 p.m. Patty still had some time before Annabel would eventually give in, allowing Liang to go back downstairs. Would he make it downstairs? Would he be waiting for Patty there as he'd said he would? She counted the ticks of the hazard signal, a ticking that made her feel as if she were moving forward and standing still at the same time. She tipped her head against the window. The night had sapped the office garage mustiness from the glass. She would call Liang back after the TV program ended.

• • •

When Patty woke up, only a few windows glowed with TV light. The ticking seemed to come from under her skull, as if her mind was projecting the flashing red lights onto the dumpsters in front of her. An ache started from her neck and grew more acute as it reached her tailbone. The roof of her mouth itched. She fumbled for a glass of water until she realized that she was touching the passenger seat, not her nightstand.

The time was 11:48. The time was not supposed to be 11:48. There was something about the time that seemed to carry a bad omen. She was not only late again but later. Latest. Cursing, she headed back, roll-stopping past flashing red stoplights, past restaurants with chairs stacked on tables. In some houses in Huntington Villa, timed lamps next to uncovered windows cast rooms under the artificial chiaroscuro of furniture stores closed for the night. On Plimpton Court, sprinkler-wet grass slavered in the moonlight.

Patty had reached the point where she could pull into her garage without once looking at the face of her house. But tonight, the house sat on a different axis. She parked in the driveway and walked to the front door. The door was like any of the others in the neighborhood, fiberglass and foam painted over to resemble mahogany. Through the thin panels on the door that were meant to give the appearance of stained glass, she saw the light from the lamp on the hallway table, and Liang's untouched set of keys. The one change was the welcome mat at her feet. It had moved. Or been moved. She would not have noticed, but for a faded corner of brick, a lighter shade of red where the mat had been.

Even the engineer in Patty held on with a tenuous grip to the predictable superstitions—leave a fan on overnight and you could die in your sleep; call your son a dog and he'll grow up happy and healthy as a puppy. Patty did not know that less than thirty minutes ago, her son had followed his sleepwalking sister back into the house, this time closing and locking the door behind him. But the sight of the mat, and the WELCOME angled sideways, made the scene look like a warning. And so she asked herself: Did something happen?

Inside, the house felt vast. Empty. She did a mental check of what was supposed to be there. Early holiday cards still lined the top of the piano she never played. Scuff marks at Annabel's height ran along the walls of the playroom. The roof was high, the legs of the living room sofa spilled onto the sheepskin rug. Was everyone where they should be? She was about to call upstairs when a murmur reached her from the far end of the L-shaped downstairs hallway. She hurried to the room. At the foot of the bed, the blankets her parents had gifted her for her wedding night had bunched together. She climbed onto the mattress and hovered over a pair of familiar legs, thick and bare and uncovered. "Liang? Everything okay? I wonder . . . the kids, I will check—"

"No . . . come to bed. Huh, uh . . ." Her husband's voice lurched forward. "They're fine." When she moved closer he quieted. Heat rose from his legs. His hair tickled the inside of her wrist, his words melting back into sleep. "Don't wake them—please . . ."

Patty watched the outline of the man. How heavy his chest looked, how hard it seemed for a big-bodied person to breathe. The first time they had had sex, months after their wedding and a whole year after she'd spent the night at his studio, she'd assured him that it was okay, stilled him when he vibrated with indecision. *One year*, she thought as her eyes adjusted to her husband. One year had felt long enough to fall not only in love but through it. And to come out on the other side with a child. How time warped her former self, turned her inexplicable.

Now here they were again: one fucking year without fucking each other. One year that felt now like one sleepless night, somehow too long and too short at the same time. She looked down at Liang's face, his straight line of a face, oblivious. During the day, he was aggressively alert—a falter in Annabel's step and he was there, prepared for a disaster Patty had not even considered. There was nothing to worry about. He had been home, after all. She was the one who hadn't.

Liang had fallen back onto his pillow, his arms fanned out toward the edges of the bed. Her tailored skirt was bunched at her waist. She crawled toward his face. If a stranger had suddenly sneaked into their backyard and peered through the one open curtain, she would not have stopped. Better to be seen by a stranger than by Liang. She hoped he would not open his eyes for a while longer.

She followed his scent—something fishy, maybe spoiled. Was this a dream? Could you smell in a dream? If she knew that she was in a dream, she could control the dream. She could mold her husband. She had the freedom, in this maybe dream, to press into him, sliding forward until she wedged her head in the groove of his neck and felt him between her legs.

She was doing it. She was on top of him, pinning his legs between her knees. If she believed that there was nothing to fear then there would be nothing to fear; she could stake her claim to this illusory body and rock back and forth. She rocked back and forth. Her husband mumbled a *huh* or an *ugh*. His body contracted and stiffened, as it often did at her first touch. She grabbed his chest and flicked his nipples. Pulled at his loose collar, wrestled his shirt over his head. She could feel him getting harder. Then there was the fumbling, her fingers meeting his at his underwear's waistband, the two of them trying to do the same thing and getting in each other's way. There was no logic in dreams. At night Liang was the impulsive one, which made Patty's scant moments of impulsiveness appear exaggerated. For once, she wanted to drag his underwear off and rake her nails far too hard down his back. And she did. With his eyes still closed, Liang winced—perhaps she was hurting him. She brought his clump of fingers to his mouth, her mouth. There the fishy smell was strongest. *Of course*, she thought. *Those hands made dinner.*

She kissed the hands and threw them on the bed. She moved down from his chest. Liang muttered her Chinese name. *Qīng-Qīng.* To the untrained ear the words could slide into a plea for gentleness, qīngqīng yīdiǎn'r, as her teeth grazed a scar on his side. Liang sighed as she shook out of her skirt and the rest. His eyes were still closed as she touched herself, her fingers coming away slick. They did not open when she climbed back over him. *Fuck*, she said, at first to a familiar pain. Her thighs chafed against his. *Fuck—fuck—fuck.* Soon they found a rhythm. *Fuck,* she said to the clap of their bodies. Was it an order? An interjection? In English, all words could soar, could pirouette. A word could mean anything. Liang lay still, but then the sharp edges, the hard *ck* chipped away at him. The word goaded him on. His heart pounded through his hands and he shot up, knocking his face into hers. Now he was awake. Or was she the one awake? Who was dreaming? Liang palmed her open mouth. He pushed the curses back down her throat. *Qīng, qīng*, he said. *Shhh.* Patty could no longer speak. The smell

71

of her husband had become the smell of the room, of her, she could not tell the difference. She lost track of his skin, her skin. She fell into him, and when she touched his face she wondered if she was touching her own.

Afterward, she lay next to him, listening to the drone of a mosquito. An invisible hand seemed to be flinging the insect into walls. A ping, a few seconds of silence, then the whining would start back up.

Liang pulled a blanket over their chests, shielding their bodies from the pest. He tapped Patty's feet with his and laughed, though about what she did not know or ask. Of course he'd been awake the whole time, Patty thought. She'd been awake, too. How wild they'd been, how loose. She nestled closer to him.

"You missed your poker," she said.

She could see the rises and dips around Liang's jaw. Her eyes had adjusted to the dark, and she could see his face, wide and flat. A drop of light sat on his nose, which twitched a little, as it did when something vexed him.

Then he exhaled, his breath warm against her face. "I told you—no poker for me, not tonight," he said. She could hear the muscles of his jaw tightening; she could feel him smile before she saw it. "Qīng-Qīng. You read my email, yes?"

The tenderness in his voice drew her in, even as it sounded rehearsed, as if he'd steeled himself for this moment. Patty knew how to read the signs when he was upset with her: the way he emphasized the first word of a phrase and lowered his pitch, curling up the ends of his sentences as if in mocking imitation of a Beijinger. Surely he'd looked forward to the few hours every month where he didn't have to take care of Annabel. Patty cherished her early mornings and Liang prized his poker nights, and she had stolen this night away from him. Yes, thought Patty. The issue here was that Liang had missed his poker.

"You were . . . stuck in traffic," Liang said.

He did not state it like a fact. Without thinking, she thrust a finger in Liang's mouth and traced the worn edge of a molar. His tongue squirmed around Patty's finger. The mosquito zipped by her ear and she pulled her hand away, just as Liang's teeth clamped shut. She traced the cushions of his body, until her middle finger, nail chipped from biting, brushed against the hairs between his ass. Liang let out a soft, baby yelp, pulling his body away before letting it settle back into her finger.

It was the first time she'd tried something like this. Now that they'd had sex, it seemed they could keep going. If she kept her finger in his ass, the dream could keep going. It was a ridiculous thought, Patty knew, but she kept her finger there.

Now she was saying sorry to him. She meant it. Her finger met his warmth, and he clenched and unclenched around it.

"I should have been at home," Patty said, in English.

She wanted to say that she *could* have been at home, but the mosquito flew by and Liang reached behind him and wrenched her finger out. For a second, she wondered if he was about to bring the finger to his nose and smell it. Instead he took her arm below the wrist, at an angle that was a few degrees from turning painful. His thumb pressed against a vein.

"There was the crash," she said. Patty thought about the moment on 75 when the highway seemed to magically clear up. She imagined glass getting swept up before she got there, the shredded skin of a tire. "One of the worst accidents. You would not believe it."

Liang's hand was still around her wrist. A sense of danger crept up on her, though she did not know from where. A single faulty circuit, among millions of functioning ones, torpedoes an entire system. She wanted Annabel here. She wanted Annabel to be between them again. "I ran into Hal Crawford," Liang said. "Outside, getting mail. He had come back from a banquet. Somewhere nice, uptown. Anyway, he did not say anything about a crash."

Breathe, Patty thought. "I did not know you talked to the neighbors."

"Anyway. You are here now."

"I am going to check on the kids." She got up and reached over the side of the bed for her clothes, but Liang drew her back.

"You've had a long day." He lay a palm on Patty's chest, insisting that she go down, down. "Stay. I will take care of them."

74

Patty's entire body tensed and locked. What if in her absence, after years of her pitching the children off to him, Liang had seized all rights to them?

"Please, Qīng-Qīng. Stay."

Was it a command?

Her legs moved first, ahead of her mind. With a force that she had not anticipated, she kicked, sending the blankets tumbling to the ground. Liang looked dazed as she punched her way back into her work blouse. He croaked out another *stay*. Less a command, but a pleading.

"It will only take a second," she said.

As a child, Patty had helped her mother lug vegetables back from the market. Even with their hands full, the two could dodge taxis and buses and beggars without losing a breath. While Patty's two older brothers studied for the gāokǎo and another studied to get into an after-school class that would help him study for the gāokǎo, Patty and her mother walked. They took long routes past old homes from which a three-story Pizza Hut would one day rise, held their noses to the dead fish knocking against the banks of the not-yet-beautified Hai River, ran tree branches along the walls of the hútòng that would soon be razed, the ghosts of its snack stalls and dumpling shops revived for tourists in the nearby street mall. Sometimes the two walked so fast, men with their shirts rolled up over their sweaty bellies snapped at them to be careful. Grannies raised their canes as if to smack them. Patty and her mother moved, thinking not of the dust they'd accumulated behind their knees or the smell of insecticide on their skin, but of the fact that they had finished making breakfast before they left, and when they returned they would have to begin on dinner.

Now as Patty climbed the stairs to her children's rooms, she thought of her mother, falling behind her one morning on their way home from the market. Patty had been about Jack's age then. She'd walked ahead at a brisk pace, the voices around her receding, and when she'd come to the eight-lane intersection, she'd crossed without stopping. When she checked behind her, her mother was gone. She waited for three cycles of the stoplight, three waves of cars, and still her mother did not show herself. Waiting, lulled by the sound of traffic, Patty was struck by a strange and sudden realization. If she wanted, she could not only walk, but walk away. She could leave her mother. The prospect did not frighten her, nor did it sadden her. She felt a nudge of pride, knowing she could do it. And when her mother magically reappeared, frantically waving a cucumber from across the eight lanes, Patty thought: *Oh*. She waited until her mother caught up, for the inevitable scolding, but that day the possibility of leaving wormed into her brain, became a solid thing to hold and consider.

She would learn later that the farthest distance energy travels is not across space but time. While her mother and father merged into the same person, sitting by the window, Patty would imagine being the one to erect the new buildings in the neighborhood sprouting up around them. She did more than imagine. At school, she became the bookish girl who never wasted a word. When she opened her mouth, she intimidated her teachers with her assertiveness, and the boys who bullied other girls gave her a wide berth. In her final year she received better marks on the gāokǎo than any of her brothers. She was one of the rare women in Nankai University's physics department, a fixture at the top of the class. It was in that role that she'd posed with the rest of her graduating class, on the last week of school. She'd even gone home with the photographer. Yet here Patty was now, outside the closed door to her son's bedroom, scared to go farther.

From the other side came the rustling of pages. She could picture Jack sitting up in bed reading, but could not for the life of her picture what he might be wearing. It had been over twenty-four hours since she had seen him. In her mind, his room was already on its way to being historic: *The Adventures of Sherlock Holmes* tented on Jack's lap, piles of laundry at the foot of the bed, which he would absently sort through with his toes while reading. One corner of the room dimmer than the others, due to a dead bulb that he would probably change before she or Liang got to it. His knees would be bent at an angle that made his legs look skinnier than they already were. He sat up with confidence. Limbs like fork tines, she told the other mothers and fathers, but strong, grown-up bone tissue.

Patty couldn't hear the pages turn anymore. She took her hand off the doorknob, feeling a shock of shyness. Had the boy noticed some movement outside his room? Had she startled him? She had interrupted him at an hour when children believe they are truly alone in the world. She had waited too long, and if she went inside now, he would know that his mother had been standing there for minutes, deliberating. She would talk to him tomorrow.

Across the short hallway of family photographs was Annabel's room, already looking like dawn in the floor-glow of the safari animal nightlights. Annabel lay stomach down, unmoving. Patty sat beside her daughter and swept a hand over a damp spot on the mattress where the girl had drooled. The teachers at Plano Star Care had suggested Annabel sleep alone in order to expand her *circle of security*, but to see her little girl in bed was to tighten Patty's own circle of security—to wonder, always, if Annabel was sleeping or dead. Babies, she knew, deposited carbon dioxide in the folds of sheets and hollows of soft mattresses, then sucked the poison back up their little noses if allowed to sleep on their bellies. Annabel was already five, but Patty still insisted on a firm mattress. If there was a silver lining to Jack's having been far away for so long, it was that distance had spared him the onslaught of her fears.

Patty turned Annabel over, a hazy mass. She went to where the nose should be. There was a smell that reminded her of the sea. A distant pocket of breath, followed by a sound that could have come from a conch shell. Patty let out a breath. She thought of the lulls during her conference calls, when all she could hear was Raj, Karl, Chethan, and Pranav breathing. The wave-lapping comfort of that sound, even hitched with static.

Then Annabel mumbled. She turned away, mumbling some more, and Patty leaned closer. "Quit it, Elsie," she heard the girl say.

"Bǎobèi," Patty whispered, shaking the girl a little.

"Quit it. I don't like it. Go away, Elsie!"

Patty drew back, as if Annabel had been talking to her. But no, the Elsie that Annabel was yelling about was that so-called friend from school. The girl who last week had given Annabel a drawing of an exploded head, adorned with Crayola-red blood. A "gift," Annabel had called it, when she brought it home to show Patty and Liang. Liang was the one who always picked up Annabel at school, and he'd put off speaking to the teachers about Elsie for a month. Well, Patty thought now, it was time someone did something about this Elsie.

"No Elsie," Patty declared out loud.

Annabel appeared to shudder in response. Patty joined her on the bed and let her daughter roll into her. Annabel mumbled something into Patty's chest, and finally, after a few minutes, her lips stopped moving. She lay on her back, her body still.

Patty lay beside the girl's mouth. An exhale. Shadows from the hyena nightlight cut across the ceiling. After Annabel's breathing eased back, a familiar whining started up. Wasn't it too late in the season for mosquitos? Had Patty been hearing things? *At an hour like this*, she thought, *the mind takes its own detours*. She might wake up the next day and forget that she'd pounced on Liang in bed, only to abandon him there. Or she might remember it differently: that Annabel was having another nightmare, and she had stopped it.

Light sneaked inside. Somewhere inside or outside her head, the insect's whining continued. Annabel clung to Patty, the way she usually clung to Liang. Patty felt itchy and hot, but she did not move. She could not tell whose stomach was groaning, her empty one or her daughter's full one. She tried to find a place to put her arm, to bend her elbow, without disturbing Annabel. They stayed like that until they grew used to the ways they fit and the ways they didn't, until sleep gave Patty no choice but to let go.

3

When Annabel woke up that morning, she believed she was falling. The room was thick-bright and weighed down with heat; it seemed the comforter had grown as heavy as an adult overnight. She could close her eyes and give in to the weight, let the sandbags of heat push her through her mattress and bedframe all the way underground, to China.

She had not yet considered how one person's underground could be another's ceiling. How the sound of grinding steel below her did not come from China, but from Daddy bullying carrots and cauliflower into her favorite puree. Nothing lived past the open slat of her door. The column of light, the blurry, indistinct shadows were blips in wallpaper. After failing to squirm free of the comforter, she peered over the edge of the bed.

"Are you awake?" came a voice behind her, wading through the heat. A breath that was not her own, pulling her back. Already she could feel the air attenuating, her eyesight catching up to her thinking. Māma sat at her bedside. Her tired eyes jiggled in the light. She leaned away from Annabel, even as her words tiptoed forward: "Hello? Bǎobèi?"

Of course Annabel was awake. She looked straight at Māma. Maybe what Māma meant to say was, *I wish you weren't.* Annabel knew that through forces out of her control, she was giving her mother a raised skunk tail of a look. She could not see her face past Māma's reflection on the long mirror, but she knew it. Most of the time she could not see her face except in other people's faces, and now Māma's had balled up like a roly-poly intent on defending itself. If she wanted, Annabel could reach over and squash that face to China.

But that was not what she wanted. It was a school day, and Māma was home. In the morning. On a school day. Māma was in the house and not in India, talking to her and not to a phone. She reached for Māma's cheek, unable to grab on to it the way she could with Daddy's. Maybe all that talking on the phone had hardened Māma's jaw. She looked away from Annabel, toward the open door and the grinding steel beyond it.

"Are *you* awake?" Annabel asked her, giggling and tapping

Māma's cheek. *Clunk. Clunk.* "Your makeup's all dirty." When Māma did not giggle back, Annabel folded into the bed, wishing to take back the comment about her makeup. A dream tape of the night before played in her mind. She had been walking outside and Jack had refused to release her arm. Or was it Elsie? Annabel pulled and pulled and after she pulled free of whoever it was, she found herself in bed, with Māma beside her. No, Annabel was in bed the whole time. She was *dreaming* about walking outside. She tried to rewind the dream tape, but the pictures were fuzzy.

She picked up Māma's left hand and turned it around in the light. The Thighmasters and Pasta Pro cookers on TV revolved on their own by some kind of magic, but after Māma's hand turned to a certain point, Annabel had to turn it back. Māma watched her do this as if the hand Annabel was turning did not belong to her. The ring on her ring finger seemed to suck in the skin around it. Annabel leaned toward Māma's palm and licked it.

"Háizi," Māma said, her hand recoiling. She would not look at Annabel, focusing instead on the open door. Annabel's saliva on Māma's palm gleamed in the light, and as Māma got off the bed, she wiped the palm over her shirt.

Then, like that, Māma had left the room. Annabel pictured the hallway outside the door, the open room that Daddy called his office. Māma disappearing past the plastic table with the crayon stains. It was easier to imagine a space where Māma wasn't. Her footsteps faded down the stairs. Annabel was ready to resign herself to another breakfast without Māma, but all of a sudden, her voice returned. She was much louder than usual, even in Chinese. Her voice rose over the grinding noise in the kitchen.

"We're awake! Awake! Are you happy?"

The grinding stopped.

"Annabel is already late for school. I am not sure you realize."

"So you wake us up, just now. With a blender."

"I only wanted to—"

"Help? So helpful you are."

In the absence of the grinding noise, Māma's voice took on another timbre, as if it were not Māma but the house itself scolding Daddy for his thoughtlessness, treating the house as if it were only his when it was *Māma* who had made it possible to have this house and the industrial blender that had scared them both awake. And did she also need to mention this so-called *friend* of Annabel's, who haunted their daughter during the day *and* night? No wonder Annabel sleeps terribly these days, Māma said. What was Liang going to do about *Elsie*? What did he *really* do when Patty wasn't home?

"Qīng-Qīng. What do you mean by this?"

"I mean, I cannot know what happens when I'm not here."

"Then maybe you should be here."

Annabel readied herself for Māma's retort, but the grinding had resumed. Over the noise, they yelled and yelled, and the house rasped and moaned. Annabel wanted to burrow underneath the comforter, but it was too hot. Was this what being in China felt like? She did not see Māma storming off to put on clean clothes for work, nor did she see Daddy spooning his daughter's comfort snack out of the blender. She hurried out of her room and into Jack's. She climbed over the rumpled sheets and hugged a pillow that was propped against the headboard. Her brother was gone. He had to go to school today, but for some reason she didn't. Annabel made a phone with her hand and brought it to her ear. On the other side, Jack's steady voice.

Lucky you, he said.

Before Annabel could make her own luck, Māma had made it for her. During Annabel's mǎnyuè, Māma had gathered the Chengs in the dining room—newly reconfigured into a playroom—in order to begin the one-month ritual. Kneeling into the foam puzzle mats, she teased out a finger from the baby's puffy hand, guided it to the baby's heart, and pronounced "Ann-nuh-bell." Then her Chinese name, "Xiǎo Qiàn," for a modern beauty. To Annabel, the familiar woman's voice acquired an edge, and she cried.

"Oh, no," Māma said. "I am here." She lightly rocked the sleeper chair, then guided Annabel's hand to her own heart, to the breast that Annabel periodically hunted down. "Māma," she said, no longer to teach Annabel something. She said it as if to convince herself that the word meant her.

Then she brought Annabel's finger over to Liang's open hand and said "Daddy." The air around Annabel was charged with a new, alien feeling. "Daddy," Māma repeated for the girl, tracing the lines of her husband's palm with their daughter's stubby finger.

Annabel watched the two shapes above her. They smiled and basked in a happy haze of their own uttered names, and didn't notice at first Jack coming in through the swinging kitchen door, bearing an electric hair clipper across both palms, as if it were at once fragile and heavy.

"Thank you for getting it," Daddy said, drawing the object into his hands, where it transformed into something smaller. He rarely said Annabel's brother's name out loud. When he did, *Jack* sliced through the air, like an act of aggression. Jack had picked the name for himself, after plugging *Titanic* into the VHS player during one of the afternoons when he was left alone in the apartment. Now Māma guided her finger toward him.

"Gēge," she said. It was easier for Māma to say *big brother* than it was to say *Jack*. Māma had three big brothers in China, three of Annabel's jiùjius. *China*, baby Annabel had heard from time to time. *China*, which to her was a sound that her mouth couldn't make, rather than a place she had never been to. In China, you shave your baby's head after one month so the hair will grow out thick with fortune for life.

"Gēge," Māma said, gathering Annabel out of the sleeper and into her arms, closer to her big brother, to the hair clipper in Daddy's hands. *Gege* made Annabel giggle, but the buzzing that now came from Daddy's hands made her scared. It was a Bad Thing.

Jack crouched behind Daddy, while Māma sat cross-legged and firmed her hand under Annabel's neck. "Qīng yídiǎn'r," Jack said. "Màn yídiǎn'r," Māma said. The two spoke in hushed tones so as not to upset the Bad Thing. Their skin tingled as the clippers met the first wisps of Annabel's hair, and though her luck was growing, she let out a whimper.

"Stop," Māma said in Mandarin. "Something is wrong." Māma swayed Annabel in her arms, letting a sprinkling of hair fall to her knees. Jack stepped out from behind their father and sat on the mat beside Māma. Annabel's brother had not cried at his own mǎnyuè six years ago. He had not known that in another month, his mother would depart for the States, or that his father, half a year later, would surprise everyone by going there, too. Now he brought his eyes so close to the hairless spot on Annabel's head he could sniff her.

"You're so brave, Mèimei," he whispered to the top of her head.

Annabel stopped whimpering; seeing this, Daddy loosened his grip on the clipper. He had not shaved his own son's hair on the boy's mǎnyuè. His parents-in-law had delegated the task to one of Māma's brothers, whom they trusted more. With Annabel, though, Daddy would not relinquish the clippers. He found his grip again and choked it, and his hands remained steady.

The buzzing returned, and another patch of hair came off. When Annabel leaned away from the razor and into Māma, Daddy did not slow down. The clipper stopped just short of the scalp. He worked over Annabel's crown down to her hairline and around her ears. Thin piles of hair formed on the mat. Jack brushed a few strands off Annabel's face. To calm her own nerves, Māma hummed a slow, flat tune that her mother had made up when there was nothing but revolutionary songs to sing. Everyone looked at Annabel. What was she thinking?

She wrinkled her nose, and her mouth shot open.

Before Daddy could press on, Māma reached for his arm — and Jack did, too. Together they held Daddy back, anticipating a sneeze. It could arrive at any moment. All it would take

was one jerk of the neck to send Annabel's head into the razor—
and then what? Anything, everything. Daddy sat stunned, perhaps as much by the two people holding him back as by the
impending sneeze, and the three waited.

They waited like that for a while.

Annabel got to skip school the one time, and only one time.
The next week, in the days leading up to Thanksgiving break,
Māma left for work and Daddy dropped Annabel off at Plano
Star Care as usual. It was when her parents were both in
the house that something changed. The atmosphere became
meaner, sharper. Māma staggered through the garage door
with groceries that no one had asked her to get. Before even
setting down the bags, she'd strain to pick up trash from the
TV stand or plod off to the laundry room to turn off the light
that Daddy had left on. Or on the nights that she was running
late, Daddy now insisted that they wait on Māma before eating, even though the sauce for the Coke chicken would turn to
jelly and the steamed eggs would lose their steam and Māma
would come home mad that they had waited.

Pay the school bill? Daddy would ask.

Remember the teacher conference? Māma would ask.

Too busy with work? Daddy would ask.

Too busy to take care of our daughter? Māma would ask.

Their questions cut like accusations, even when directed at Annabel: Bǎobèi, any trouble at school today?

Because if there was trouble, Māma said during one dinner, Annabel should tell them, and Daddy should take care of it. And if Daddy still doesn't want to take care of it, Māma will.

"But I didn't get in trouble," Annabel whined, and Māma smiled and shook her head, and Daddy frowned and shook his head, and Jack kept eating, as if he was the one who'd gotten in trouble and didn't want anyone to know.

By the third dinner that week, a silence had fallen between Māma and Daddy. A louder silence, as if they were screaming through the house, HEAR HOW SILENT WE ARE! As the three got ready for bed that night, the silence turned solid, as if a stranger had squeezed onto the mattress with them.

At least Annabel now got to sleep with her parents downstairs again. As she lay between them, relishing their sweet skin smell, she thought how maybe the silence was not because Māma and Daddy were angry at each other but because they were scared. Daddy was scared of everything, Māma kept saying. Customer service, waiters, homeless people, not to mention Annabel's teachers. But he *had* asked to meet with Elsie's parents, Daddy reminded Māma, he had done what she'd wanted him to do. And what do you know? The teachers had told him—and quite frankly, he agreed with them—that he was *overreacting*. Meanwhile, Māma was scared to let the matter go, scared to talk about anything other than Elsie or Plano Star Care or how she'd blown most of her savings sending Annabel to a school with *incompetent* teachers who did things teachers in China would never do. Scared to the point of forgetting everything else. Like trying to make Annabel sleep upstairs.

Not that they needed to revisit that idea, thought Annabel. She slipped under the comforter and crumpled her eyes shut. Never mind if she didn't get to give either of them her one hundred kisses. The important thing was to have sweet dreams, to not wake up kicking her parents and give them something besides Elsie to fill the silence. Annabel had missed the cool sheets, all that space for her to stretch and grow. Here there were no other rooms other beds other countries other planets for Māma and Daddy to go when her eyes were closed. She would take it. And there was Jack, above her. As her parents nodded off, Annabel stared up at the ceiling and imagined his feet walking there. She imagined so hard she heard actual steps.

But Jack had come not from above, but from below. He had dug himself out of China. If you stabbed the earth with a shovel, you could peek down into China. At five years old

Annabel believed this, though she knew she shouldn't. However deep China lay, she was both relieved that she had never been there and envious that others had. She had a vague memory of dunking her face into a supermarket lobster tank and Daddy hauling her home, straight into the closet in the guest room. There were no clothes there to keep her company. She sat in the dark for what felt like her whole life, until she realized she could cry her way out of it. The closet had been frightening enough, but the closet had been no China.

Jack, however—Jack had gone to China. Which was to say, Jack was full of experience, of dark wisdom. His stories Annabel believed without question. Vampires can't go into your house unless you invite them in. Ghosts won't go away unless you learn how they died. Bad guys with guns can't see you if you're under a table. China was the land of bad guys, and Jack had been one of them. Over the phone, Annabel's faceless grandparents always ordered her to watch out for her dǎodànguǐ brother, the one who'd made life difficult since he was in Māma's stomach. They'd told her how Māma had been forced to be cut open, so Jack could enter the world. Not to mention that, before Māma went to America, he'd bite down on her nipples until they gushed with blood. It was around then that Māma would snatch the phone away.

One night almost a week after she returned to her parents'

room, Annabel got out of bed while they were sleeping and headed upstairs. She needed to seek out Jack's wisdom. As much as she liked being in Māma and Daddy's bed again, the silence there was making it harder for her to fall asleep. Annabel wanted to ask her brother if that silence had come from somewhere. Was it China? If she could figure out where the silence belonged, maybe she could figure out how to send it back.

Before she got to Jack's room, she ran into him.

"Annabel?" Jack stood in his pajamas in the narrow upstairs hallway. In the dark, he was a floating head, his big, all-hearing ears glowing in the light from his room behind him. "Are you . . . awake?"

Why did everyone keep asking her that? "Are *you*?"

Jack moved closer, and his tired face uncreased, came into focus. "I heard you on the stairs," he said, sounding less curious than disappointed. "I thought . . . I thought you were asleep."

What a strange thing for him to say. If Jack had heard her on the stairs, why would he think she was asleep? She wanted to knock-knock on her brother's head, but she was still too short to reach. "You're being in-comp-uh-tent," she said.

She wasn't sure if she was using the word right, but she liked the way it sounded. Whatever Bad Thing *incompetent* meant, Jack did not look impressed. "You don't get it," he said, and moved away from the light. She realized her brother was evaluating her—like Māma, whenever she asked Annabel about Elsie. "Why're you here, anyway? Go back to sleep."

"I tried. I can't."

"You get to sleep in Mom and Dad's bed, and you can't?"

"The bed . . . it's *different* now."

Jack glanced back toward his room. For a second, she thought he was going to ask her if she wanted to sleep with him. Most days Annabel could barge into his room, but something about Jack now made her feel like a vampire, like she needed an invitation. If only he knew that she would follow him anywhere. Then her brother turned around, and the creases on his face returned, more pronounced. "You really don't remember walking outside?"

"But Gēge. I'm always walking."

"I mean, at night." Jack placed a hand on her shoulder, which felt like another thing he'd picked up from the adults. "Late at night. Last week. Don't you remember?"

Now Annabel was wondering if they were still on the same team. She shook her head, but Jack kept asking. "You got all the way to the bridge. Why can't you remember?" Annabel shook her head harder, feeling the contents inside swish around like the car passing by their house—she could hear the *swish, swoosh*—as Jack continued talking.

"Maybe you do remember. Maybe you're pretending."

Sometimes Annabel would pretend to be invisible, or dead. Daddy would tiptoe like a T. rex into a room, and she would hold her breath under the bed, watching the hair on his toes. Monster Daddy could sniff out the fear that little girls sweat, but Annabel was so good at not being afraid that sometimes their games took forever and she gave herself up. She'd cough, and Daddy would pull her out from under the bed and throw her over the bed, and his fingers would scurry under her arms and over her belly as she wheezed through laughter for him to stop, and then he would stop, though she did not really want him to.

Now she wanted Jack to stop. "I don't like this. You're mean."

"*I'm* mean?"

"I'm just a little girl."

Jack smiled, though he did not look pleased. Maybe his smile had gotten older, too. "You love being the little girl, don't you? Pretending to sleepwalk so Mom and Dad can wake up and think, where's our little girl? Where's our bǎobèi? Well, too bad. Guess I was the only one who noticed."

The more Jack pressed on, talking more to himself than to her, the more Annabel wanted to cry. Only she didn't want to do it here, so she laughed.

Jack frowned. "You think this is a joke?"

"Gēge," she said. In that dark hallway, flanked by framed shadowy photographs, Annabel had trouble standing. "I want to go home."

"What?" Jack inspected her like a puzzle.

"Home. Home. Homehomehome—"

"Okay—okay."

They were finally agreeing on something, but on what? And why didn't it feel like agreement? As her eyes adjusted to the dark, Annabel took stock of her brother. She *was* just a little girl, and Jack—Jack was not yet an adult. A child like her, even if he'd dug himself up from China. Whatever it was he'd accused her of, she could get back on his side by saying she had done it. He knew more about the world than her, anyway. Mummies in Egypt have hearts, not brains. Zombies in China don't walk, they hop. Little girls in America don't always get what's real. "I'm sorry," she said.

Jack smiled. A kid's smile. "Look—"

"I did it, Gēge. I'm sorry."

Her brother's face twisted, then softened. He seemed to recognize something in Annabel, just as Annabel was recognizing something in him. He crouched down and met her at eye level. He brought a cold hand to her, which made her realize that her cheek was hot. "Forget it," he said. "I think I'm just tired. Let's go back. I'll take you there."

. . .

"You're going to be in trouble," Elsie said the next day, squinting up at Annabel.

Perched on the top of the monkey bars of Plano Star Care, Annabel swung her legs over the edge. From her vantage point, it looked as if she were kicking Elsie right in her shiny forehead. She wasn't—the girl was too far down, and the bars too high up—but still she liked to pretend.

"I really, really don't want to be in trouble," said Elsie.

Two boys scampered past the girl, kicking up pea-gravel dust onto her sunflower-printed dress. Annabel laughed as Elsie patted her dress, only to get dust on her hands. Elsie's face had turned the same shade of red as her hair. She raised her palms to the sky—to Annabel.

"It's the last day, and I only need three more stickers until I can get a gift prize, and I've been saving up *all year.*"

Elsie and her stickers. Her sticky and sparkly treasures, those assorted blue jays, cardinals, swallows, and bald eagles. She needed two more to complete her flock by the beginning of Thanksgiving break. All Annabel had asked was for the girl to join her up on the monkey bars, as a condition of being her friend. Elsie had protested, because she had to be good to get her stickers.

It wasn't that Annabel wanted to make life difficult for

Elsie Louise-Defliese. If anyone wanted such a thing, it was Māma and Daddy. As long as Annabel told them what they wanted to hear about Elsie, she could sleep in their bed. Annabel actually looked forward to seeing Elsie's sweetly puckered face. The best thing about Elsie was that she never gave Annabel orders. Since August she'd attached herself to Annabel as if Annabel were a wise and wizened middle-schooler.

Of course, Elsie's devotion could be too much. She'd wait for Annabel outside the bathroom, or follow her around at recess as if Annabel had grown a tail, and sometimes Annabel would get fed up and order Elsie to quit it, and sometimes it took awhile for Elsie to listen. But she would always listen. She would always follow. There was a pleasure to having a person who trusted you unfailingly, who clung to you for every direction: not only did Elsie believe the words that came out of Annabel's mouth, but Annabel had started to believe them, too.

"Hey, Annabel! Can you . . . *please* . . . be careful?"

Annabel stood on top of the monkey bars, her feet teetering where the bars intersected. She could see cars speeding past on the other side of the fence. A customer filing out of the AutoZone and into the Korean donut shop. Miss King's sun hat and Miss Dreyfus's bald spot.

"Oh, no! Hey! You'll hurt yourself!"

Annabel considered the ground. After a certain point, distance can appear an abstraction. For months, she had felt compelled to jump. The lone consequence seemed to be a good one: the ability to have a lime green cast decorated with her admirers' signatures. An invisible force heaved toward her, a voice from Down There that told her *do it, do it*.

She plucked out a strand of her hair, let it drift to the ground. Her body stayed still.

After a few more seconds, she crouched down and wiggled her body between two bars. Hands clasped to a bar, arms stretched so far she felt her bones growing—finally growing— she pointed her toes toward the gravel, and hung there before letting go. A perfect landing.

"Not today," she said to Elsie. "I'll break my arm after Thanksgiving."

"Do you . . . have to?"

"I got to do it before Christmas. Then Santa will give me a big and beautiful cast greener than Kermit. And you can put your stickers on it."

Elsie was on the verge of tears. "But I wanted to put my stickers on my lunch box."

"Hey." Annabel was almost a head shorter than Elsie, but when she brought her hand up to the girl's face, Elsie winced. "It hurts so so so much to break my arm. I'll feel better with your stickers." Annabel gave the girl's cheeks a light sweep. "You're my friend, right?"

Now Elsie Louise-Defliese was looking down at her Mary

Janes, as if she were concentrating fiercely. Annabel glared at the girl and made a cup with her hand, bringing it below Elsie's left eye and blocking her view.

"Hey, Elsie," she said. "If I catch one single tear, you're going to be in trouble."

Elsie sniffled. "*You're* in trouble. You're giving me a bad touch."

Annabel's eyes darted reflexively to Miss King. On the other side of the playground, Miss Dreyfus was in the middle of teaching a calligraphy lesson in the sandbox. Earlier that day, Miss King and Miss Dreyfus had sat everyone down for a Serious Talk. Annabel knew it was Serious because Miss Dreyfus didn't make them giggle by speaking French.

Daddy's good-night kiss is a good touch.

Mommy's big hug in the morning is a good touch.

A high five from a friend is a good touch.

A doctor checking our tonsils is a good touch.

A teacher taking out our splinters is a good touch.

A crossing guard pulling us away from a fast car is a good touch.

A good touch should never be a secret.

A good touch should never cross Down There.

Their parents were also going to receive a letter, Miss King and Miss Dreyfus had said after the lesson, a letter that explained how having Serious Talks about Serious Things can be Seriously Hard. Just because something is hard doesn't mean it's not useful, they said. If we can understand what a good touch is, we can understand what a good touch isn't.

"Like a bad touch?" someone had asked.

On the playground, a few kids had crowded around Miss King as they waited for their turn to try on her sun hat. Annabel waved in their direction; no one waved back.

She turned to Elsie. "You better stop *overreacting.*"

If Annabel could understand what an overreaction was, she could understand what an overreaction wasn't. Elsie protesting Annabel's orders for once, as she was doing now, was an overreaction. Elsie holding back her tears, her eyes throbbing with fear, was an overreaction. Annabel grabbing Elsie's arm and yanking her behind the revolving tic-tac-toe blocks, out of view of both teachers, was not. So she did it. She yanked.

Swings creaked behind them, and a boy whose skin burned on his way down the elephant-trunk slide broke out in sobs. Miss Dreyfus hopped out from behind the elephant's rear to attend to him. "*Pardon! Ça va, mon petit?*"

"You're hurting me," Elsie said.

"Friends can't hurt other friends," said Annabel.

"But it *hurts.*"

"Then I guess we're not friends."

Annabel looked down at the hand that clasped Elsie's arm. She hated that something so small, like a doll's hand, could belong to her. At least with Elsie, Annabel's hand could produce real effects. Snot streamed from Elsie's nose in a glistening, spidery line. She issued a pathetic whimper. Annabel zipped up Elsie's lips with her other hand. The girl was like an injured beaver sniffing for air. Annabel had never seen a beaver and mixed them up with hamsters. Sorry little creatures trapped in cages, going round and round and round.

"Elsie? Did you hear me?"

The girl shook her head.

"That means you *did* hear me, dummy."

"Sorry. I'm really, really sorry."

Elsie's voice dropped to a whisper, even as Annabel pinched her arm harder. Elsie's insides had gone quiet, too: her arm lay slack, and her eyes stopped bulging.

"I'm not a good friend," Elsie said.

Instead of quailing in fear, she just seemed tired, like Jack that night in the hallway. Ready to give up her arm to break in place of Annabel's. It wasn't fun, seeing Elsie like this.

Annabel tried to smile. "Maybe if you give me your stickers—"

"No," Elsie said. "I shouldn't be your friend."

Annabel dropped Elsie's arm. Between the tic-tac-toe blocks, light slanted across Elsie's palm. Annabel's only friend had released adult words in the air, and now nothing was fun.

"I'm not good enough! So I won't be your friend."

"Don't be a dummy," said Annabel.

"Dummies shouldn't be your friend!"

Annabel saw herself coming back to school after Thanksgiving break, sitting alone on top of the monkey bars during recess and looking down at the tops of heads, none of them bothering to look up. Now she was the one who wanted to cry.

The tears on Elsie's cheek were drying. There were the red indentions of nails on her arm. Elsie eyed Annabel with an expression that Annabel, for the first time, could not decipher. On the other side of the tic-tac-toe blocks, Miss Dreyfus and Miss King announced to the children that it was time to go inside. Sneakers crunched against gravel.

Elsie looked down, Annabel up. The girl's words had set Annabel off balance, and it seemed both of them struggled to stand straight. Each took notice of the other's mess of hair, the half of a shirt collar upturned. They waited until it seemed the world had returned to normal. They needed the world to be normal if they were to be special.

Elsie rocked back and forth demurely. "Or maybe . . ."

"Maybe don't be a dummy and stay my friend."

The words had tumbled out of Annabel, and when she saw Elsie smile, she could not help but to match it, three times as big.

"You mean it?" Elsie said.

"Stay my friend, always and always."

Elsie brushed her nose with the back of her hand, leaving a trail of dirt above her lip. She made sure to wipe the snot off on her dress before taking Annabel's hand. "My arm doesn't really hurt, anyway," Elsie said.

"Duh," Annabel said. "It was a good touch."

Threading their fingers together, they passed the tic-tac-toe blocks and slides and monkey bars to fill the final two spots behind their classmates. This was how it would be, thought Annabel. Always and always.

"Late, girls!" Miss King said as she marched down the line, the brim of her sun hat bouncing. "What if we left y'all here? How would you feel, Annabel Cheng? And you, Elsie Louise-Defliese?" Their teacher's smile somehow widened as she said this, and the rest of the children sneaked gleeful glances at Annabel and Elsie behind her. "Eyes forward! Eyes forward!" ordered Miss King, and the children resumed formation. From the front of the line, Miss Dreyfus counted them off, *un, deux, trois, quatre.* Smudges of sunlight caught in people's hair, and sweat stuck onto necks. There were necks, so many necks, between Annabel and the open door. When she checked behind her, she saw that Elsie was looking back, too.

4

Before Liang Cheng became a father, he had been, briefly, a son. His mother died, and he lived with his father and his father's father in the Shaanxi country-side. During summers, the plum rains pulled down the sky. They fell in drops so big he could dodge them. While Liang danced around the rain in the courtyard, his father slept. Thunder and leaky ceilings did not stir him. With enough yellow wine, he could sleep for days.

At five years old, Liang did not flinch when his grand-father whipped his father with a willow switch to rouse him. Each lash made him stronger, his father said. He also kept a pail by his bed to catch the treasures from his stomach. His breath carried the smell of dead philosophers. He slept hugging a flute carved from the bones of an ancient red-crowned crane. The flute, he told Liang, was over eight thousand years old. Like tea steeped in red clay pots, its sound had grown rich from all the sounds that had passed through it.

Never mind that the instrument was as light as bamboo, that Liang caught splinters when poking his finger through one of the holes. It was enough to sit by his father and listen. The man never looked at Liang for long, but he didn't shoo him away.

"Your mother lives on the moon," he told Liang one night.

"But the moon's right there," Liang said. "I can touch it."

What Liang saw outside was a guardian, a friendly face over the hulking Qinling Mountains. He knew this moon better than his mother. The woman had played flute for the Liberation Army, his grandfather had told him. During one of their marches she'd met his father, a team leader whose speeches inspired fellow peasants to work until their bodies broke. The two were an auspicious pairing, entrusted to lead China into its future. But days after giving birth to Liang, his mother slipped from the hayloft in the old communal barn and landed on her neck. Now his father was the one who looked back.

"Your mother is alone up there. All night she talks to a rabbit." He spoke as if narrating a dream. "Don't believe your grandfather. Your mother left us. It was her choice."

If Liang were to ask his grandfather about the moon, he would probably say that the dark spots looked less like a rabbit than his father's vomit on the floor, the vomit he'd order Liang to wipe up. The old man didn't see dragons in the clouds or rivers on his palms. But when Liang was in his father's room, he wanted to go where his father went.

Before Liang's mother lived on the moon, his father continued, she'd spent many nights with his father, hiding in the communal barn. Back when the two had not yet married, the hayloft was the only place where they could steal a moment alone. While horses slept below them, their tails swishing dust up to the rafters, Liang's mother spoke of leaving their village. They could tour bigger cities, venture into other counties, wading through marshland, camping under the starry desert sky; wherever they stayed, whether it was in the factories of the north or the mud houses of the south, they could inspire their people, she said, with her music and his famous speeches. Liang's father offered a silent assent, though in truth he liked where they were. He lived with his father. He had responsibility here. But he loved Liang's mother. During rainstorms, he listened to her play her flute in the barn, a tune she'd invented for him, a sound only he could hear, and he thought how if he had to, he would march farther than any soldier for her— he would follow her until his feet turned to ash.

Liang wanted to warn his father, to stop him before he

went on with the story. This will end badly, he wanted to say. It was dangerous up in the hayloft, especially during a storm. Maybe that was why the commune had torn down the barn in the first place.

His father went on. He and Liang's mother eventually met with the county magistrate. They were armed with convincing arguments: morale was low across China, people thought the grain quotas were too high, and who knew where such whispers would lead? It was time to shake the peasants out of their fantasies, to get their hands and feet moving four times as fast in the name of the Party. To their surprise, the county magistrate agreed. He would send them out with a traveling theater group after the harvest. Liang's mother rejoiced.

Then something happened.

"What?" Liang said.

"You," said his father.

Before Liang could take shape inside his mother, the two sought permission from the Party to marry. Gone were the days of firecracker-paved wedding processions and sedan chairs; Liang's mother and father were wed in a mass ceremony with fourteen other couples, though the Party strategically placed them in the center. Soon after she moved in with Liang's father and grandfather, Liang's mother began to change. She fainted coming back from the well. She fell asleep on the threshing floor. She lost the energy to play the flute.

Nights trying to sleep over the wood-plank bed, she dreamed of maggots eating her insides, of roots growing from her feet and lashing her to the ground. The longer Liang's father stayed by her side, the more he felt himself sinking into the muck alongside her.

Before long, he grew desperate. After consulting in secret with a village grannie who still carried on with the old beliefs, he traveled west until he found a woman known as the Queen Mother. He had come right in time, the Queen Mother said, from the entrance of the cave. She was leaving this earth soon and had two vials of healing elixir left. "One for you and one for your beloved. Drink and reclaim your strength for all eternity," she croaked. "But be warned, my womb has run dry. These elixirs are the last of their kind."

The story was beginning to take a strange turn, Liang thought.

His father returned to his mother with the two vials sealed in his pocket, the crust on his eyelids lifted, his lips breaking out of their crooked mold into a sturdy curve. He appeared stronger out of mere anticipation. They would return to being model peasants, he informed Liang's mother. All they had to do was drink the vials together, and they and their future child would never tire in the fields. The three would turn over a new world. They would not need to leave when they could make this place a paradise.

SIMON HAN

Though his wife struggled to sit up on the bed, he thought he caught a spark in her eyes. That night, the two returned to their hayloft, though they no longer needed to. Liang's mother even played the flute, a mournful melody that moved his father so much that he suggested they wait one more day to drink the elixirs. The county magistrate had permitted him to tend to her while she was sick, and he did not want to return to the fields just yet.

The next morning, a stranger met Liang's father by the well. Speaking in an unfamiliar accent, the man explained that he was a messenger for the Party. The immediate presence of Liang's father had been requested. Word had spread about his rousing speeches, and the Chairman himself wished to meet him. After seeing the invitation in Mao's own writing, Liang did not hesitate to accept. While Liang's mother was sleeping, he departed from their village wearing his most humble peasant's tunic. He imagined his face alongside the Chairman's on the posters. He spent weeks in Beijing, behind the gates of Zhōngnánhǎi, sharing stories of backbreaking work in his home village, his words soaring and spiraling from his mouth. He never met Mao, but the Chairman's highest advisers licked up his every word. When they invited him to stay for another year, the temptation to say yes burned his mouth. In the end, he declined with a heavy bow. He had a family, a paradise to build.

At last, he returned to where he began. He slipped into their village under cover of night. No one was home, so he investigated the backyard furnace, where his father and the other villagers were pulling an overnight shift, feeding the kilns with what appeared to be pots and pans from the communal kitchen. When he called for his wife, the other villagers cursed at him. What a scoundrel for running off, they said, and while she was in so vulnerable a state!

A realization came to him then, and he dashed away to the barn, which was strangely emptied of horses. He climbed up to the hayloft. There, a baby lay swaddled at the edge of a makeshift straw bed, under a horse-size opening in the roof. He hurried to unwrap the baby, thinking it was choking. In his arms, the baby looked like a rooster with all its feathers plucked. It was a boy. His face, wide and enigmatic, was the spitting image of his father's.

Hugging Liang to his chest, his father felt a pulse. A softness. He held in his arms a fragile thing. He felt a fragile fear. It was then that he spotted, buried in a nearby pile of hay, the two vials of elixir he'd left with Liang's mother. Opened and emptied—both. He peered out the roof, following the path of light. Standing before Mao's advisers, he had taken care to look down at his feet. Yet now he saw her: Liang's mother suspended in the sky, drifting toward the clouds.

What kind of healing was this? What kind of strength? He

had hoped only for her to smile again, to be able to shoulder the carrying pole, to work. "What have you done?" he yelled. His cries scared Liang into silence. They tore the villagers from their work and summoned Liang's grandfather to the barn. From her great height, Liang's mother could not hear them. She could not see them. She had taken the light for herself. Clouds draped over her body, and like a plume of smoke she mounted the air until she was no longer of this earth.

In his room, Liang's father turned away. He held Liang's mother's flute to his chest. Maybe that was why he slept so much, Liang thought. The man needed to rest, to prepare for the day when he would see his beloved again. Without more elixir, he would have to resort to yellow wine until he was strong enough to fly up there as well. The furniture was broken, the walls molding, but his father could not be bothered when he was waiting for something better.

Liang waited for his father to fall asleep. Heat sat on the man's eyelids. Liang took off his shirt and slipped into the sliver of space behind him on the bed. His grandfather had probably fallen asleep in their room next door, because he did not call for Liang. He spotted a mole at the base of his father's neck, and he wondered if he had that mole, too. Maybe if he fell asleep with his father, he could dream his father's dreams.

When his father woke up later that night, Liang woke, too.

He could feel the hot air from his father's mouth, still pungent with wine. His father inspected Liang. He took his chin in his hand. "Where is she?" his father said. Liang looked outside, at the full moon: soon it would be the Mid-Autumn Festival. His father looked on with his head tilted, which made Liang wonder if his own head was the one tilted. "Why can't I see her?" his father cried. "Why don't you look like her?"

When Liang tried to edge away, his father grabbed his mother's flute and, without warning, smashed it against the windowsill. Liang gasped and tried to save the flute, but his father held it out of reach. He pointed the broken end toward the window. "She's gone. You've got none of her in you." Then he hunched over and became quiet.

Liang had to lean in to make sure he was breathing. It was as if he had one foot in a dream and another outside of it. The man in front of him did not seem real, and yet if Liang touched him, he would be. If Liang's mother really lived on the moon, he thought, he would snatch her from the sky. He would take the moon, too. Ships would crash into bluffs, owls would flop out of trees, and the sun would never rise again. That would be fine.

He leaned closer to his father. He told him not to worry. One day, he would grow bigger than his father. He would travel the world and beyond. He would find his mother, no matter how far she was, and bring her home. By this point Liang saw him through a haze. He felt a little brave. To reassure his father the way a mother might, he bent down and kissed the rim of his ear. The man's breath caught. He opened up and gathered Liang in his arms, cradling him as if a head or leg might topple to the ground.

His arms brought Liang closer. Something was wrong: he was too close. "You know why she left?" he said, his breath hot and sticky above Liang. Pressed against his father's chest, there was no room for Liang to shake his head. The flute had caught between the two of them, the cracked end scraping against Liang's side. He preferred his father when he was in a story. "She left because of you," he said.

The splinters from the flute bit into Liang's skin. His father's body muffled his voice. When Liang squirmed, his father held on tighter. Years later, in those moments when Liang's heart would beat out of his skin and he would reach for the nearest object to hold and crush, he would remember the force with which his father had held him. How he needed Liang to buoy him, to guide him back to shore. How Liang had begged him to let go. *Bà. I can't breathe. Bà.*

His mother had left. She had chosen to leave. She had gone so far she had forgotten her son below. Soon the moon she lived on would shrink to the size of a fingernail. Oceans would roil with her beckoning. Mountains would peak in a failed attempt to reach her. But whether Liang tried to fall asleep on his father's pillow, stuffed with old clothes; in Tianjin in a studio he shared with four other men; or in Plano, Texas, on a mattress engineered to remember the weight and shape of the bodies it held, he could reach toward a window and coax his mother onto his palm. He could convince her that his hands *had* come from hers. Stay here awhile, he could say. Everyone else would soon be gone.

Tonight the moon was missing. As Liang stumbled home from a game of poker at Jerry Huang's house, he searched the sky. That was what all the photography books written by New Yorkers ever mentioned about the state: *That big, gorgeous, mythic Texas sky.* He had never understood the concept of a Texas sky, never bought into its vastness. Was it any bigger than the sky in California, or New York? It had seemed much smaller than the skies he remembered in China, even the ones punctured by the skyscrapers of Tianjin.

But tonight the moon was missing, and the sky had never seemed so big. Big and blank and interrupted by roofs and satellite dishes and crosses. Starless and full of folds, blue-black hiding spots. Liang's shirt clung to him with sweat. He imagined the wind ferrying warmth from the Panhandle, swirling with the evaporated salt spray of the Gulf. How long it had been since he'd breathed the air with conviction. There was no such thing as a Texas sky; there was only sky. What made a sky a Texas sky were the things on the ground, which he ignored in order to look up. There, the new lawn of an over-eager neighbor, with gridlines separating square patches of fresh, breathing sod. There, an American flag in a backyard, too heavy to sail even with the breeze. Jerry's neighborhood sported houses with advantages over Liang's that were apparent only to those who lived in either community: barely wider driveways, more numerous balconies, a suggestion of larger space between houses. The obvious difference was the Christmas lights. It was not yet Thanksgiving, but here they already webbed the streets, a grand show of participation. Liang's eyes were only now getting used to them.

Maybe the moon had moved. Maybe it realized it wasn't needed anymore, with all these other lights. The sidewalk squares of the Huangs' community vibrated with their shadows. Rainbows reflected in puddles. How many sidewalk squares would it take to get back home? Patty would know. She'd have the foresight to estimate the average number of sidewalk squares in one square mile of residential Plano. Liang didn't even know how many miles away he lived from Jerry's house, only that it had taken ten minutes to drive there.

Now to walk home, in a place like this. None of his photography books had mentioned the unused, Christmas-light-lit sidewalks of Plano, Texas. A suburb of sidewalks leading away from low-stakes, in-home poker games. Liang's group had met at Jerry's house two hours ago, playing behind open blinds on tables where the scent of household cleaner lingered. None of them had smoked since China. The beer cost more than the buy-in. Poker was less motivating than the idea of having something to be motivated by. On their children's Thanksgiving break, they huddled over beers and pistachios.

Liang had not even wanted to go to poker night. He'd skipped the last one for Patty, and this time it had been Patty who'd convinced him to go, to show up. *Get out of the house. Do something.* What was the point? In a few days, his poker group would be at Patty and Liang's house for a Thanksgiving potluck, guests at a party neither Liang nor Patty wanted to host anymore, yet they continued to plan for it, out of a different kind of obligation, for to cancel a party was to announce to your guests that something was wrong.

Of course, nothing was wrong. Nothing was wrong, Liang had reminded himself, growing restless during the poker game. At some point, he'd wandered back from Jerry's kitchen, his seventh or eighth beer in hand, to the sight of four slumped bodies and heads around the low-lying lamp, and he'd wondered if in his absence they'd magically departed from the house, only to forget to bring their bodies.

Then Michael Wang, a Taiwanese acupuncturist, picked up a few chips and placed them, in his slow and deliberate fashion, in the middle of the table. Dechao glanced off in the distance before inspecting his hand again. Zhuping, with the shortest stack after Liang's, shuffled his remaining chips until one of them rolled off the table. Jerry folded his cards and kept them in his hands, his eyes glazed in the direction of the front door, probably wondering if his daughter, who was living at home again, would be coming back at a reasonable hour. Liang had heard about Jerry's daughter dropping out of college from Dechao, the stocky owner of a battery company, who jawed with the surliest of Chinese businessmen overseas but whose two teenagers lectured him in public on his English. Liang and Zhuping had shared a laugh once about Dechao's nasty children, though Zhuping had them beat, with a son whose medical condition compelled him to go on pornography websites at other people's houses without even trying to be discreet. Liang had no idea what condition that might be, only that it was Michael who'd told him—Michael, who was unable to get his wife pregnant, though she desperately wanted to be, his wife had admitted to Patty, in a separate moment of indiscretion. (The Wangs were going to *therapy*, Liang had heard from Jerry, whose own wife, Helen, was holed up somewhere upstairs, or not in the house at all.)

Maybe something was wrong, Liang thought. These men

had bodies like storm-battered palm trees. They were wobbly men who made sturdy moves in the game, only to go home and become wobbly all over again, snoring into their wives' turned backs, waking up their children for hugs they did not wish to give. And Liang had become one of them. Or worse: Liang had always been one of them. What was it Patty had accused him of doing the other day? *Hiding.* Not from anything in particular, just . . . hiding. The kind of father who would rather endure his daughter's suffering in private than fix what troubled her in daylight. *Will you do something now?* she'd demanded of him again last Friday, after Annabel reported that Elsie had invited her for a playdate over the break. *What kind of bully invites over his prey?* he'd asked. Could a five-year-old be so nefarious?

You don't know, Patty had said, *why we cling to the people we do.*

Some days, Liang would stare at Annabel and wonder what she was capable of. Plano Star Care talked of *activating each child's unique zones of potential,* but would it not be better if there were nothing in Annabel to switch on? No surprises as he watched her grow day by day, year by year? Yes, better his daughter be capable of nothing, not even dying. Better to be a bag of shiny rocks. Liang had believed the teachers when they'd assured him that nothing was going on between her and Elsie, that the girls stuck to each other like flies on honey (neither of them were flies, they were both honey, they hastened to clarify). The teachers' assertions seemed more palatable than the possibility that Liang could have come so far only to raise a child who, like him, continued to live in the shadow of danger. Impossible. That was why he and Patty had moved here, was it not? To be in a place where such dangers were impossible, could not even be conceived of . . .

Then there was Annabel, too, a small human with an outsize imagination. There was no reining hers in, so Liang did what he could to direct it. Better to convince the girl of her own superhuman strength, her ability to make it in a world that she liked to pretend was treacherous. *Be scarier*, she always told him. *Stab me harder!* There was a benefit to playing the monster in their father-daughter games: the more Annabel believed she was in danger, the more she would also believe in her ability to survive it. In the end she always won, the monster sentenced to prison in the pantry, or withering into dust on the carpet. Lesson learned. To convince a child that she was invincible: what more could a parent want?

Patty had been right about one thing, though. Liang *was* hiding. When he returned to Jerry's poker game with the beer, all this became clear, even as the numbers and shapes on his cards were starting to grow blurry. He was hiding here in his big wobbly body costume, wasting away with four other wobbly men instead of going home and doing what needed to be done. No more sending his wife embarrassing, emasculating emails. He would confront her directly: the problem wasn't some little girl they didn't know. The problem was that the people he did know, the people he loved, were all going to leave him one day. Convincing his wife to sleep with him and arguing with himself about what to do and not to do about his daughter were half measures. His father had liked to talk but never got out of bed. If Liang wanted to keep his family, he would have to be invincible himself. *Do something,* as Patty had said.

What was Liang supposed to do? For starters, finish this beer and get out of this house. With a three and seven in his hand, he went all in. When he showed his cards, the other players looked at him as if he were joking. Instead of sliding his last stack across the table to Zhuping, Liang made them topple over into a mess of colors. Luànqi bāzāo. The other men offered to let him buy back in—*only ten dollars, just for fun anyway*—but he staggered to the living room and tore his jacket from between the sofa cushions. His friends trailed behind him, taking turns meekly offering him a ride. Liang waved them off as he tried to find the openings in his shoes. *You're not driving, are you?* they kept asking. It was too far to walk, someone mentioned, but no one repeated the offer of a ride. Pathetic as they had become to him, he could not help but feel a little disappointed that no one had been more adamant.

Outside, the air was finally cool enough to soothe his face.

He followed the path of Jerry's tulips, lit up in red and green. The lights made him squint. In December, there would be fifty-dollar horse-drawn carriage rides and a slow file of vehicles from other neighborhoods weaving in and out of the streets and cul-de-sacs. The exteriors of these houses would be turned over to visitors, while the families themselves disappeared behind the brick-and-stone veneers. The rides at Montmartre had become a Cheng Christmas tradition.

From the sidewalk, Liang looked at the men. None had crossed the garlanded frame of the door. He said, "Annabel always asks us to set up lights."

Were they nodding? He couldn't see their faces.

He said, "I should actually set up lights this year."

He wasn't sure they'd heard across the lawn. "I should!" he shouted. "I should! I *should* . . ." but as he spoke he forgot what it was that he should be doing. Why was he leaving poker night so early again? Where was he supposed to go now? Propped up against the doorway, his friends might as well have been dead men. Jerry looked especially corpselike, the way his head bent sideways and stayed there. They still looked wobbly, but not in a pathetic way. He imagined taking their pictures like that, four bodies slumped together by the door. They had one another at least. He hoped they would come to his Thanksgiving party.

Before Liang could speak, Jerry raised a hand. The rest of

the men waved, too. Liang glanced back toward the street, wondering if the men were waving past him, toward the house that faced Jerry's. A house that resembled Jerry's, which in turn resembled Liang's, except the neighbors here had set up a Nativity scene on their front lawn.

The plastic stable swayed in the wind. It felt nice, the wind. Above the sodium streetlight, another light winked across the sky in a straight line. An airplane? Where were the stars? Where was the moon? Liang turned back to the men to say something about flimsy baby Jesus being scared of the dark, to lighten the mood before inviting himself back in, but then the door had closed, leaving the silhouette of a wreath.

When the moon used to go missing, Liang would suspect his grandfather. "Where have you taken Māma?" he'd ask. "Give her back—I'll call the authorities!" He would have been Annabel's age then, a small, loose-limbed dǎodàngui. His father was gone, too—mining coal in the Qinling Mountains, his lungs already hardening into two black, iron weights. It would be years before Liang would see him again, shrinking on a hospital cot at the base of the mountains in his last, angry days, his voice too hoarse to tell any more stories.

This is what Liang remembered, walking back from Jerry's

house: dogs howling in the courtyard as rain struck fur. The air smelled of mud and trash from the cornfields. On humid, moonless nights, it became harder to breathe. Alone, his grandfather did nothing to expand the walls around them. He carried the pocks and creases of history on his face, but no photographs to remember Liang's parents, to set against altars of incense and fruit and candy and watered-down liquor. At least Liang could see his father through his grandfather: the same dramatic slope of the shoulders, tapering off to smooth and hairless arms. He could look at himself, too: with a mouth and belly that resembled his father's, Liang always looked *full*, the other villagers would say. What was the boy filling his stomach with, if not his father's yellow wine?

You and your father. You and your father. No one ever mentioned his mother.

"Do I have her eyes? Her nose?" Liang would ask his grandfather at dinner.

"Quiet," the old man would say. "Food's getting cold."

Here, now, Liang's mother's moon still evaded him. He searched for it on Plano's main roads, the ones with island medians. He walked farther from the low, castlelike walls that surrounded Montmartre. Many of Plano's residential communities were enclosed by stone walls, even if they didn't boast gated entrances. Anyone could come and go as they pleased. The walls serve an aesthetic, or perhaps a symbolic function, a categorical separation of neighborhood streets from city roads.

Cars passed without slowing. Liang could not remember the last time he had driven at this time of night and seen someone walking down this businessless stretch on Legacy. Maybe he had also passed them without slowing.

He tried to count the sidewalk squares and kept losing track. It was hard to count sidewalk squares when he kept looking up. How was it that a sky so sprawling could offer so little to see? During this hour of the night when nothing moved forward or backward, he could have crossed one hundred sidewalk squares or one thousand. At some point Plano Star Care manifested around a corner, the featured business in a familiar strip mall. A banner under the school's illuminated sign read LITTLE GENIUSES WELCOME.

He stopped, as if to see where his feet would take him. To his left, on the other side of Sheridan, past a long field of clovers, would be Logan Elementary, Jack's old school. Next to the school there would be a playground and another stretch of machine-fed blackland prairie, and beyond that an enclave with a small pond where Liang had once spent an afternoon with Jack.

Yes, he had once spent an afternoon there with Jack. The boy Patty called her jīn gǒu. He'd sat on the bank of the pond with him that day, trying to clear the fog between them. One oak tree had burls bigger than his head. Another had fallen, the break from the trunk shaved white like a husked coconut. There was something reassuring about the place, about being led there by Jack. Still, all these years later, Liang could not remember what the two of them had talked about that afternoon. He could not imagine a single line from the conversation they'd surely had. At some point, he'd stared at his son, trying to recognize himself in him. The boy did not have his eyes or his nose, Liang had thought to himself. He did not have his father in him at all.

Now it dawned on Liang that it had taken him all night to even think of Jack. He'd been so fixated on how to prove himself to Patty and what to do about the Annabel problem that Jack had hardly crossed his mind. As Liang made his way past Plano Star Care and the path that led to Logan Elementary, this realization sobered him. Scared him. He tried not to think about what he hadn't thought about as he finally turned in to his community. Hints of moss climbed up the section of the wall where the name Huntington Villa was engraved. He looked above the Neighborhood Crime Watch sign, but still no moon. Between the houses, no moon. Of course, his mother had never lived on the moon. She'd become, as he learned in primary school, another iteration of myth. The moon goddess Cháng'é drank the world's last two elixirs of immortality, consigning herself to an eternity of watching bodies warring from the night sky. In some stories, she became Chairman Mao's late wife, the first of many martyrs to die at the hands of the cruel Guómíndǎng. And Liang's father? Not the victim, but the villain.

Cháng'é, Liang's mother. The first person to leave Liang, which made her, in a twisted way, the person he felt closest to. If he could remember his mother as anyone, even as a stain on the moon, then she could always be around.

Only now she was gone. Really gone. Maybe that did make her the villain. *Your mother left us,* his father always said. *It was her choice.* Liang turned onto Plimpton Court, his melancholy sharpening into anger. What had he done to deserve these blisters on his heels? His mouth was so parched he was tempted to lap up the spray from the sprinklers he passed. He wobbled up the cobbled pathway to his house, only to discover that his keys were not in his pocket. He must have left them at Jerry's. The others had probably tried to call him. Where was his phone?

He tried the backyard instead. Maybe Patty had left the back door unlocked. How easy it would be for anyone to do this, he thought, as he unlatched the gate.

The backyard was the one space in their house that he and Patty had left largely untouched. The crabgrass had the same off-yellow tint during all seasons, a familiar Velcro texture. One fourth of an acre so bare even the rabbits didn't visit. Why had he bothered having anyone cut the lawn?

Liang crossed over the grass. How would it feel to leave it tall, dandelions tickling his shins? He had a sudden desire to take off his shoes and socks, to feel with his bare feet. If the back door wasn't unlocked, he would sleep out here, looking beyond the tapered ends of the fence planks, each one pointing to a different cluster of stars. He would wake up to the moon fading into daylight.

When he tried to bend down to reach for his shoe, he lurched forward, almost falling to the ground. He gathered himself. Why were his shoes wet? There was a figure by the back door. The figure moved closer and became Jack.

"Dad?" The boy was wearing his pajamas and his mother's slippers. Liang wondered if he had come out to join him, to sleep under the stars together. Then he saw the concern on Jack's face, a kind of concern too old for a boy, and he knew that Jack had come out to retrieve him.

"Oh," Liang said. But wait. He was not the kind of father who staggered home every day with the front of his shirt drenched in beer and fire in his eyes, the person you had to throw a blanket over when he plopped stomach down on the couch. Whatever Jack was seeing, it wasn't right.

I was looking for the moon, Liang wanted to say.

"I can't find my keys," he said instead.

Jack put his hands in his pockets, as if the keys might

somehow be there. Then he took his hands out. "You could've used the doorbell."

The boy must have known why Liang hadn't. That was why Jack was lowering his voice, his mother and sister sleeping on the other side of one of the shuttered windows. *Don't be embarrassed,* Jack seemed to be saying with his eyes.

"Mom was worried," said Jack.

"Nothing to worry," said Liang.

"Don't you want to come inside?"

"Yes, but . . ." Liang shifted his weight from foot to foot, his shoes making wet, squishing sounds. He had a vague memory of walking into a puddle right before coming here, formed from the mix of sprinkler runoff and one of the leaking trash bins a neighbor had wheeled out to the sidewalk. If only he could get these shoes off. He tried and failed again to bend over. There could be nothing worse than falling in front of his son. He stared at his shoes, as if willing them to come off. When he looked up, Jack was smiling.

"What's so funny?"

"That sound. It's like your shoes are farting."

So this was what Jack saw in him: not a shǎzi—a child. A farting cartoon of a man. Liang's son, treating him as if he were his wayward little brother. Jack was coming closer. A dim light enveloped his face, and Liang did not need to look up to know that the moon had finally made an appearance. As he watched Jack's narrow eyes come into focus, his regal nose, a realization came to Liang. He did not know whether to be awed or horrified by the thought, only amazed that it had never before crossed his mind. It was then that the boy crouched down and reached for one of Liang's shoes, and Liang recoiled and slapped his hand away.

In the quiet, the slap reverberated. It had been a long time since Liang had heard a sound so loud. The slap had sent Jack's arm swinging, and as if in one fluid motion, Jack rewound his arm and dropped his hand to his side. Liang could see Jack's other hand crossing over and rubbing the spot where Liang had touched. Slapped. A tiny slap. The boy was acting as dramatic as his sister did, and for what? To make his father feel worse? Liang's hand was not a willow switch. Other parents slapped butts, even faces.

He thought of apologizing, but to do so would be to make all this a bigger deal than it was. Jack seemed to have already recovered, standing before him. The realization that had come to Liang was that Jack did not look like him because he looked like Liang's mother. A woman neither of them had ever seen.

Yes, that was Jack. Jack was his mother. And here was little boy Liang, plopping himself on the grass. He yanked at the laces, then pulled at the shoes without untying them. Eventually he got them off. Jack backed away, as if waiting for Liang to turn back into the father and give him permission to take his leave. Just as Liang was about to give it, Jack asked, "Something to drink?"

"Beer?" Liang grinned, but the boy did not laugh.

Inside, Liang lumbered over to the kitchen and drank straight from the faucet. Jack was in the middle of taking a glass out of the dishwasher but Liang waved him off. He went back for another gulp from the faucet, and another. Jack looked on as if he had something to say. He put the glass in the cabinet and stood there.

"Go back to sleep," Liang said.

"Okay. Cool." As Jack walked away, he muttered something else that Liang did not catch. Jack could not go back to sleep because he had stayed up all night waiting for his father, but Liang did not know this. He listened to the boy's soft thumping steps and thought how it was past his bedtime.

By the time Liang got his pants off and flopped into bed, the nightstand clock read 1:45 a.m. His head throbbed and the red numbers stared out at him with judgment. He considered waking Patty to tell her that he was back. Or maybe Annabel, so the girl would say *Daddy, Daddy*. It would be nice to hear that, especially now. But the two lay next to each other sound asleep, and they did not move.

Patty and Annabel would leave him one day. Jack would

leave him one day. When the legendary archer Hòu Yì watched Cháng'é drift away into immortality, had the archer considered that his body carried behind it the gust that sent her off in the first place? That he was the reason she was leaving?

A flap of the heavy curtain had been pulled back from the window, revealing the soft box glow from the moon. Liang thought of walking over to take a closer look, but the sheets were cool, and the bodies on the bed were warm. There was nothing he needed to do for now. When Patty woke up in a few hours, it would be her first day off from work in half a year, and she would be full of plans.

Later, in a long line to check out at Costco, she would reveal to him that she had invited Elsie's parents, of all people, to their Thanksgiving party. She had extended—what did they call it?—an olive branch. If she was going to bring up the sensitive issue concerning their daughters, she might as well do it over mashed potatoes and that barbecue pork Liang still needed to preorder from First Chinese Imperial.

"Excuse me," someone behind him and Patty in line would say.

But they would not move, not at first.

5

Jack's parents had not even prepared a turkey. They spoke of "Thanksgiving" the way they spoke of the "red" in "red light," as a word that made one thing different from another, otherwise similar thing. On the day of the party, their house announced to the others on Plimpton Court, we have company, too—more company than you do. None of the neighbors had been invited, not even the Martinezes, whose son, Marco, a school pariah ever since his failed push-ups debacle, Jack now avoided.

It had been a long fall, made worse by the general feeling that fall had not ended, and the holidays were an illusion. His parents had argued bitterly about dinnerware and whether or not to move the dining table from storage into the playroom. (Did this mean she no longer had a playroom? Annabel had whined.) Then the guests began to arrive, all of them late, some apologizing that they would have to duck out early even before stepping through the door. They smelled like the food that they'd brought, the usual Chinese restaurants.

For Jack, parents at these kinds of parties, Thanksgiving or not, all blurred into the same concoction of a person. "Āyí hǎo, Shūshu hǎo," he greeted the pairs as they shook off their sweaters and light jackets. "Āyí hǎo, Shūshu hǎo," Annabel repeated after him, until the first and only white family, the Louise-Deflieses, arrived, and his sister frothed at the mouth with excitement, she and Elsie firing language at each other that no one, not even their parents, could understand. The dǎodànguǐ Jack's mother had portrayed during her dinner table quips with his father did not resemble the delicate, church-dress-wearing Elsie in front of them. It was Elsie's mother, appearing almost grandmotherly compared to Jack's mother, who sneaked her husband an are-you-seeing-this look when Annabel grabbed Elsie by the wrist and dragged her friend, head bobbling from the force of the tug, up the stairs to play.

Jack's father sheepishly volunteered to tag along behind the girls, which prompted Elsie's father, a thin, professorial man, to more confidently take the lead before Jack's father could. Left alone with Elsie's mother, Jack's mother told her *Welcome* for the fifth time.

Jack kept count: of repeated words, questions, conversation topics. He had nothing else to do; there was no one his age at the party, though his mother had tried to act as if the four teenagers who had come with their parents were in range. There was nothing worse than introducing yourself to high schoolers as the One Who Lives Where You Were Forced to Visit. But he had to stay downstairs at least until they'd eaten. His mother had told him so—a rare order, which had made him want to heed it.

It took twenty-two minutes for his mother to announce that it was time to eat and thirty-four seconds for Jack to pack his Styrofoam plate. Adults leaned against kitchen counters and wall niches, balancing sesame noodles and chāshāo ròu over wineglasses and speaking to those whose children they recognized.

Some āyís were more familiar than others. One had been in their house many times before. His mother's version of an Elsie, with a face as wide and round as one of those Bratz dolls Annabel was always asking for. As Jack was trying to finish his food, the āyí wandered over to his corner of the piano room, one eye on him and another on his mother beside her, a lasso of questions connecting them.

"And what is yours learning now, in middle school?" the āyí asked his mother.

His mother laughed. "I think Huáng Āyí is asking you a question."

Jack wasn't so sure. Most āyís did not speak to him; they spoke about him, through his mother. What could he say, anyway? School bored him, not because memorizing facts about ancient Mesopotamia and photosynthesis was easy, but because such knowledge felt like cheap padding: second-rate, knockoff knowledge. The real stuff unfolded out of sight. All the dangers the teachers had prepared them for in those first weeks could not have magically vanished. If he could have gotten his head out of his books, he might have heard the bomb threats that Naveen Naidu had surely muttered under his breath in Honors Science, or caught the mysterious hand that had slipped inside Brett Liggett's boxers in the locker room. There was even an eighth grader who had gotten pregnant and still wore tight T-shirts though she was showing, who was debated over during lunch with an equal mix of reverence and fear, though Jack had never gotten a look at her except as a passing blur in the traffic of the hallways. Huáng Āyí and Shūshu had a daughter like that, he remembered. Her name was Charlene. He'd heard that she dropped out of UT Austin and now modeled for underground car racing websites, though he'd failed to find her with any of the search engines.

"The world," he offered to Huáng Āyí, with a shrug, "and stuff."

That was when his mother stepped in. She talked about her changing attitudes concerning private versus public, the competitiveness of Plano schools, *pre*-pre-SAT-for-admission-to-Duke-TIP classes starting in Jack's grade, maybe they should move to Frisco, ha-ha, not to mention Annabel's school! In Annabel's Montessori-inspired school, she said, the teachers treat the students as if they are both their equals and their own children. His mother's teeth were stained red, he'd noticed, as she emphasized, in English, the word *inspired*.

"Oh, how wonderful." Āyí made her wine go away. "That could go in a brochure."

"Yes, Helen. But—" His mother laughed abruptly, then filled the silence by playing with Jack's hair, something she rarely did. "Her school is like a foreign country. The children are very accomplished. They don't do childish things. This is good, usually."

Evening had settled; his mother kept the curtains open. Then one of the teenagers was directed to play the piano, Annabel's future piano. The shiny block of keys had sat untouched for so long it seemed a miracle that music could suddenly pour out of it. His mother had not protested when Jack asked to quit after a year of lessons.

The playing drew disparate conversations together, raising

the volume of the room and making it harder to hear the music itself. Elsie's mother wandered over, and talk of Plano Star Care vanished as Jack's mother and Huáng Āyí switched entirely to English. Just days before the party, Jack's mother had complained over the phone to his grandparents about Elsie's mother: *Can you believe the things she must have taught her daughter to say?* Yet now she seemed to be channeling the real estate agent who'd originally shown them around the house—*a former model house, for the developer*, his mother was telling Elsie's mother now.

"So many families once walk through this place, imagine their own house can look something similar. But then we say: why not buy the model house?"

Elsie's mother peered down, rubbed a crack between the wooden floor slat with her bare toes. "Oh, yes, I see what you mean. It does feel rather lived in."

Jack's mother drew Huáng Āyí and Elsie's mother closer. "Sometimes, I still hear them. All those young parents, with their babies. They come through that door, walk through that hall. Now their babies must be as old as my Annabel."

But this house had come with a discount, thought Jack. The first and oldest house on the street: the developers had been desperate to sell it. They'd even let them keep most of the furniture. His mother had not cared to mention that.

"Oh?" Elsie's mother said. "Was your daughter born here?"

Jack's mother smiled—beamed, even. "She can be president."

Elsie's mother exchanged a look with Huáng Āyí, one of curiosity masked by a smile. He wondered if the two knew each other. Huáng Āyí asked Elsie's mother about Elsie, and Elsie's mother asked Jack's mother about Annabel, but no one asked Huáng Āyí about Charlene.

Before long, the chatter reached that register where Jack could comprehend individual words but not sentences, not meaning, a swirl of sound that made him sleepy—for once—so he plotted his escape. Before he could reach the stairs, he ran into a different sound, men laughing, his father laughing, a living room of men laughing, in front of the Cowboys game.

"Holding?" Elsie's father asked the TV. "Refs!" He took off his horn-rimmed glasses while Jack's father and his poker group shūshus echoed with something equally incredulous. Elsie's father raised his glass of red wine, sending a splash over the sheepskin rug. At first only Jack and his father noticed the stain. The two of them stared at his mother's favorite rug, watching the stain grow, before Elsie's father got up. Jack's father shook his head, insisted that he would take care of it, but then Elsie's father noticed Jack. "Little man," he called to Jack. "Mayday. Mayday."

Then they all turned to Jack. It seemed even the referee on

TV was motioning at him. *Mayday. Mayday.* The energy in the house reached a new register. An encore in the piano room, glasses ringing in the playroom turned dining room. Somewhere, someone was singing. And before he knew it, Jack had brought over a roll of paper towels and planted himself in the free spot on the couch beside Elsie's father.

"Good sir," the man said, taking the paper towels from him.

Elsie's father, like her mother, seemed to belong to a different generation—a different time—than Jack's parents. He sat with his legs crossed, a wrist balanced palm up on the knee, as if an invisible cigarette was smoldering between his fingers. His hair seemed windblown by the years, thick and silvery, with no trace of Elsie's red. The sight of the man breaking out of his portrait pose and hunched over as he tried to clean up the stain felt incongruous to his nature. He was, as Jack had overheard him saying earlier in the night, retired. You had to have accomplished things in order to be retired.

"What's that?" Jack pointed to the man's rusted belt buckle, the faint outline of a skull-and-crossbones design. It seemed not so much old as valuable, or valuable because it was old, like something that could go into a museum.

"This, my buddy, belonged to my grandfather." Elsie's father's eyes twitched—twinkled with excitement, maybe. "He was a member of the local Twenty Tuff Tamales. That's T-U-F-F, by the way. Ever heard of it?"

There were so many things Jack had not heard of. He could watch CNN until the commercials turned to late-night infomercials, and still he could not hear it all. His father looked on, drinking his beer, as if to hide his roving eyes. "No. My grandpa isn't from around here."

"Not many folks know about it," said Elsie's father. "That's the thing about this place. No one's really 'from around here.'" As if a sudden idea had popped into his mind, he unbuckled his belt, right in front of the other men. He slipped the leather out from the loops on his jeans and handed the belt to Jack.

Jack blinked, slowly. "For me?"

Elsie's father laughed. "For the next five minutes."

The buckle was heavier than Jack had expected. He was not sure if it was okay to touch. As he shifted the belt between his hands, Elsie's father explained that the Twenty Tuff Tamales was from long ago, when there was a club for tough guys from Plano who practiced good deeds. A precursor to the modern fraternity. Jack did not ask him what a fraternity was, let alone a precursor to one. His father was looking at the TV, though Jack knew he didn't care about football. It occurred to him that his father didn't know what a fraternity was either. This, he had to admit, disappointed him.

"Can I see?" one of the poker group shūshus asked. The man accepted the belt from Jack with two hands. The rest of the poker group passed the belt down until it reached his father, who held it as if it were a rodent, then handed it off to Jack.

"Me, I don't have a son," Elsie's father said, leaning toward Jack as if confiding in him. "But I could see you joining in league with those fine young men."

"I wish I could!" Jack said.

"Well, you can. In spirit, that is." Elsie's father grinned. "You just got to be tough, and you got to be good. The first part's easy. I spent thirty-two years keeping kids not that much older than you from going to jail. I've lost at least three years of sleep trying to do it. I mean, these kids! You get them to wear a suit to court, then in front of a judge, they hurl a glass of water at their parents. They're tough, but they're not good." He rapped Jack's arm with his knuckle. "You, Mister Cheng, strike me as both."

Was it true? thought Jack. Was he both? He had an urge to run from guest to guest, shaking them and proclaiming that he was both *tough* and *good*. Then Elsie's mother spoiled his fantasy, walking—no, marching—over to the living room and asking Jack's father where the girls were. His father stammered something about them wanting to build a pillow fort upstairs, a private pillow fort, and Elsie's mother turned to her husband and said, loud enough for everyone to hear, "You said you weren't going to leave Elsie alone. With her."

Elsie's father tried to head her off—the girls were fine, fine—while Jack's father began to apologize. That was when Jack's mother joined the gathering as well, adding to the noise, muddling it. Sorry, I will get them, his father kept saying. And as the other adults fumbled to find the right words with which to appease one another, Jack remembered again: he was both.

"I'll do it," he said, jumping up from the sofa. "I'll watch them."

His parents and Elsie's parents looked at one another. It seemed they were considering his offer. Yes, let him save the party, they were saying with their eyes. With the trusted Jack watching over the girls, the party could go on. A card game was unfolding in the dining room, and didn't they want to play? And what about another drink?

One day, thought Jack, he'd host his own parties in his own former model house, and he'd make his own son be as helpful to his parents as Jack was going to be now. He swelled with pride, imagining the compliments he'd get. Already Elsie's father was leaning back in what appeared to be affirmation. Reflexively, Jack brought a hand to his forehead and, without a second thought, saluted him and the room.

No one returned the gesture. Elsie's father turned back to the TV. The poker group shūshus looked equal parts confused and amused. His mother watched his father finish another beer. Only Elsie's mother smiled back, the way she might to a child Annabel's age who was pretending to cook the adults a delightful meal.

Why had he saluted them in the first place?

Stupid, he thought, as he left the room. Stupid.

Upstairs, he passed three snickering teenage boys huddled around the computer in his father's office and barreled through Annabel's door without knocking. In the two weeks since Annabel had moved back downstairs to sleep, there had been little occasion to enter her room. The window blinds by the bed rattled and shook.

The lights were off. At first glance it looked as if no one was around. But there were pillows splayed over the floor, a mound rising and falling on the bed. He tore off the comforter, revealing a coiled-up little girl: Annabel's friend. Elsie did not move. He leaned closer; she became more still. He tried poking her.

Finally, her body uncoiled. She turned her head toward Jack and screamed.

He screamed, too. Immediately, Annabel burst into the room behind him, gesticulating wildly and stomping her feet. "EL. SEEEE. You're supposed to be *quiet*."

"But—but who is he?"

Annabel thrust a finger at Jack, with an intensity that dented the air. "Can't you tell he's my brother? Are you blind?"

By this point, Jack had turned on the lights. The two girls squinted at him, protesting that it was too bright. He wondered how long they'd been playing in the dark.

"What's going on? What is this?"

"Annabel wanted me to pretend sleep so she could come inside like a kidnapper and steal me and I'm not supposed to scream because kidnappers always say *shut-up-or-I'll-kill-you* but then you came and and and also I don't like this game."

Annabel charged toward Elsie, but Jack held her back. Something was wrong, that much he knew, though he would be able to put his finger on it only after it was too late. He was here to watch the children, he thought. That was what he would do.

"No more games," he said to Annabel, tightening his grip on her arm.

"But Daddy always—"

"No more."

Annabel kicked and glared at Elsie. "It's all your fault!"

"Your games aren't fun!" Elsie said.

"Take it back!"

It took every ounce of strength to keep his grip on his sister, whose rage sent her airborne in his arms. Elsie backed away until she bumped into the dresser by the bed, knocking down a vase with fuzzy fake flowers his mother had set up.

"Fine," Elsie said, wiping her nose. "I'm *sorry*."

After that, the tension in Annabel's body quickly began to dissipate. Before long it was gone. Jack tentatively let go of her. Was it that easy? Was she pretending?

"Okay," Annabel said.

"That's it?" he said.

"I forgive you. I mean her."

Fifteen seconds ago, the girls had been ready to tear out each other's throats. In half that time, the energy in the room had shifted, the simmering explosion congealing into something like boredom. Another fifteen seconds later, and the girls were rolling around on the bed, restless, asking him to chase them.

"Catch us!" Elsie said.

"Abduct us!" Annabel said.

"I'm not abducting anyone," Jack said.

Now the girls were united in their protests. If they whined any louder, the parents downstairs might hear. Or worse, the teenagers in his father's office might wander in and laugh at them—at him. He suggested hide-and-seek.

"Boring," Annabel said.

"Bet you can't find me," he said.

"I can too."

"Okay. If you can't find me, you got to sleep by yourself. Upstairs."

The mention of Annabel's sleeping arrangements shut her up at once. Her eyes darted between Jack and Elsie. "But I do sleep by myself," she said.

"You do?"

"Gēge. Bié shuō."

"Then turn around and count to thirty."

Humbled, Annabel tugged Elsie to the corner of the room, where they faced the wall and counted. Jack slipped inside the open closet in the same room and watched through the gap as the girls flew out to the hall yelling *Ready or not, here we come!*

Then he was alone again. Alone in his sister's closet. He grew bored himself. There were baby clothes stacked atop an already full storage container. Why hadn't his parents given them away? Were they saving the clothes for another baby? No, no. They were keeping them, like how Lǎolao and Lǎoye kept his mother's school acceptances, or that letter from Nankai University's president congratulating her for placing at the top of her class. In America everything was an accomplishment, even growing out of baby clothes.

Before long, the girls' footsteps tumbled down the stairs, followed a few minutes later by the teenagers'. A stillness spread through the room, though it was different from the stillness of most nights, when Jack tried to stay up while everyone slept.

Downstairs at the party, there were many noises to choose from, and the trick was to find the important one, the meaningful one. Jack stepped out of the closet and inched over to the bedroom door. He could make out the girls' voices, pleading with the parents to help them look. Jack was too old for such games, but he felt a thrill, knowing people could be so desperate to find him. He could hear his sister accusing the parents of lying, her indignation rising with each *I don't know* or *That brother of yours is clever, isn't he?*

Then his father's voice entered the fray. It was not one to cut through a crowd, the way it did now. It jostled the other voices for position, insisted on being heard, swinging from highs to lows as if he were singing. He was talking to Jack's mother. He kept saying *I told you I told you I told you.* I told you the girls were fine, he said. Look at how much fun they are having! Look! Then Annabel butted in. She was *not* having fun, everyone was tricking her, she was upset—no, *disappointed.* And when someone laughed, she yelled, "Tell me where he is! *Tell me! Tell me! Tell me! Tell—*"

"Xiǎo Qiàn," Jack's mother snapped, a rare use of Annabel's Chinese name. It had little effect. Annabel went on, demanding that the adults give Jack up, until their father agreed to assist in the search. Another voice—Elsie's mother's?—asked Jack's father if something was wrong, but he only grunted. His grunts trailed behind the voices of Annabel and Elsie. The three voices grew closer, louder.

They were coming up the stairs! In the hallway by then, Jack ducked into his father's now-empty office, behind an artificial tree. Some of the leaves had been stained black with permanent marker. He spotted the girls tromping up the stairs with his father lumbering unevenly behind them, a fresh beer in hand. He had gotten used to his father coming home drunk this past year, and tonight he could smell him even from across a room. Unlike his mother, Jack did not mind the smell of the beer that made his father more expressive, his movements clumsier and more childish. It made his father smaller. If his father was smaller, then Jack did not have to be in such a hurry to become bigger.

He watched the three turn the corner down the hallway, away from him. Their voices faded in and out of the bathroom, then his room. His father spoke to the girls in exaggerated whispers, as if he didn't want to give himself away. For once, his attempt at secrecy was blatantly obvious. Even Elsie was telling him to be quiet.

Eventually, the three turned back in Jack's direction. He tensed, thinking they were going into the office, but his father raised his beer in the air, halting the girls.

"Have you checked, have you checked . . ."

"Talk faster, Daddy!"

"Have you checked your room?"

Annabel giggled. "We *came* from there."

Jack couldn't get a good look at his father in the hallway, could only imagine the man's face, the realization settling into it. His father sometimes had that face—that distant, measuring look. As if he knew something about Jack that Jack didn't know himself. Maybe that was what it meant to be a father, to know your son better than he knew himself.

"Yes, yes . . ." his father said. "Follow me."

There was a thunk against the wall.

"Daddy! Be careful!"

The three made their way to Annabel's room. Once he was in the clear, Jack left the office and crept closer. The door was angled in such a way that he could see what was transpiring in half the room. His father set down his beer on the dresser before peering under the bed and nearly falling on his face. Annabel snorted with laughter as she watched him, then bounced in and out of view. Elsie peeked into the closet, where Jack had been, then entered it herself.

That was when he heard Annabel whisper to his father—a conspiring whisper. And though Jack could not grasp her exact words, he knew what she would do.

His sister walked into Jack's line of sight, though she did not notice him. She stood in front of the open closet door, swaying in place the same way he'd found her the night she'd sleepwalked outside. He had begun to doubt that the Annabel he'd rescued a few weeks ago had been in need of rescue in the first place. Had she really been sleepwalking? Could she be that scary, that she'd pretend to do so? Here she was now, plotting her next move. She covered her tittering mouth with one hand. She shut the closet door with the other.

Without delay, Elsie yelled and tried to get out, but Annabel, from the other side, kept a firm grip on the knob. While Elsie banged on the door, Annabel swallowed her laughter and pushed her back against it, digging her heels into the carpet. She flipped the closet light switch on and off to add an extra dose of misery. Of course Jack would be blamed if this went on. It was just like him to come up with the inane idea of hiding, after he'd volunteered to watch over the girls. Of course, his father would be the one to save the day.

As if on cue, his father teetered toward Annabel. He mumbled for her to stop, but Jack's sister was still possessed with glee. She reminded Jack of that Lucy from *Dracula*, and it would take more than pleading for her to go quiet in the night. Jack's father must have understood this. Tonight, his stern words or his well-timed theatrics would fail to bring his daughter back to sweetness.

Jack studied the man. What would he do? Each time Elsie rammed the door from inside, Annabel's heart leapt out of her chest. His father stumbled closer, surveying the scene, considering. At least there was no one else upstairs, no one to witness Jack's inaction, or his father's. Though maybe that was worse, thought Jack. Maybe if he revealed himself now, pretended that he'd just wandered in . . .

Before Jack could take another step, his father latched onto Annabel's wrist. His sister seemed surprised by the man's forcefulness. Surprised, but not scared. She did not budge. His father tried to pull her away from the door, and she resisted. He pulled one way, she pulled another. Finally, he used a strength that was not pretend, and she toppled a few feet into the full-length mirror.

At once, Elsie burst out of the closet. Her hair was a mess and her cheeks gleamed with tears. She took in Annabel, crumpled to the floor, Jack's father crouched next to her. "I'm sorry," he muttered. "I thought. I thought." He seemed desperate for Annabel to get up, to say something. As if in a daze, she touched her shoulder, her elbow, her head. Only then, after she realized that it was all there, her body intact, nothing bleeding or broken—only then did Annabel allow herself to cry. She cried so hard that Jack's father had to back away. Watching her, Elsie wilted, as if whatever anger she had harbored for Annabel had again evaporated. Annabel's friend was no bully, that much was obvious. She loved Annabel. She said as much now, taking Jack's father's space next to her.

"Was it . . . him?" Elsie said. She did not have Annabel's daring, could not bring herself to point at Jack's father, hovering awkwardly behind them. All the same, she dangled the possibility. "Did he close the door? Did he abduct me?"

Annabel, for all her daring, could only nod. For some reason Jack's father nodded, too. It seemed his father's head had grown heavy, and he had no choice but to nod. Jack had an urge to take the man's head in his hands and straighten it.

Elsie cried with Annabel. "Mommy always says you have bad manners and I shouldn't play with you if I want stickers. But it's not fair. Just because Annabel's daddy is bad doesn't mean she's bad. I want to play with Annabel always and always. It's not your fault. *Your* daddy's not *your* fault."

Jack could see Elsie's words worming their way into Annabel's head, reconfiguring the code that had kept other thoughts at bay. Something had tipped. The house had been built on an incline this whole time, and Jack was now realizing it. Annabel wiped her eyes; the tears stopped. She rose.

"I don't care what your parents say," Annabel said. For once, she towered over the still crouched Elsie. "You better shut your face."

"But—"

"I mean it. You better not talk bad about my daddy. Or else he'll come to your house and touch you. He'll give you a bad touch."

Elsie bristled. She did not move at first.

"A *bad touch*." Annabel repeated it simply, like a vocabulary lesson.

The blinds were closed but the lights were on, imbuing Annabel's words with a daytime quality, like a playground taunt. Elsie seemed to have been struck by them, with a disproportionate force. She could not look at Annabel, or Jack's father, and certainly not in the mirror.

She tried to back away, but Annabel seized her arm, the way Jack's father had moments ago seized hers. Annabel and their father were in cahoots again. Or were they? His father was trying to chime in behind them, issuing the smallest mewls of protest. But Annabel had the floor. She was not finished.

"You just saw my daddy do it to me," she said. "And he'll do it to you, and it'll be *really* bad. He'll go to your room one night and touch you. *Down there*."

The party downstairs had moved to a new stage, a quieter stage, and Jack could hear the slap and click of playing cards. It was from that sleepy postdinner space that Elsie at last let loose a howl. A howl that morphed into a horrible moan as she burst out of the room, brushing past Jack as if he were not there. It happened so fast he had no time to react. No time to note the slow, swiveling motion of his father's head. As if he'd noticed Jack for the first time. Somewhere behind Jack, Elsie was fleeing down the stairs, toward safety.

"I thought," his father said.

He did not tell Jack what he thought.

Elsie must have parroted Annabel's words down every step toward the adults. She must have screamed *bad touch bad touch* the whole way, as if the crime had already occurred.

A few weeks later Jack would tiptoe down the same stairs, wondering if the sound that he'd just heard from his room was that of a little girl like Elsie whimpering, or the nervous chuckle of a shūshu or āyí. But no, it was only the scratching and rattling behind the walls again. No longer calling for him, he'd realize. It was the machinery that ran the house, pipes and wires that spoke a language he didn't know. A new winter darkness had set in. One high windowpane in the living room, oddly, would be fogged up. He would remember all the breaths that had filled their house during the Thanksgiving party, all that fire and heat as Elsie catapulted toward the adults. How he and Annabel and his father had timidly followed her down the stairs, looking for any other place to be. He would remember the white glare from the chandelier, and all the other lights that had been flipped on in the house. On any other occasion, his mother would not have allowed the drain on their electricity bill. There were empty closets in empty rooms, and empty shelves in empty cabinets, but Jack would remember every door as closed, every crack filled in by light.

By the time they were halfway down the stairs, a cordon of parents had formed around Elsie in the foyer. She was slapping at the thin glass panels in the front door, and twisting the knob with such force that it looked as if the knob was twisting her hand instead. It was not enough to get away from Liang; the girl seemed desperate to flee the house altogether. No one could get through to her until finally her parents' voices pulled her toward them. "Use your words," commanded her mother. But the words Elsie kept using were Annabel's.

"He did it to me. He gave me a bad touch. Down there!"

Elsie's parents stood rooted in place, the shock not yet reaching their faces. The other parents and a few curious teenagers looked on, in amusement and confusion. What sort of performance was this?

Before long, people's lips worked themselves into motion.

Bad touch? What kind of bad touch?

He? Who was *he?*

"Elsie, baby," her father said. He crouched down, eye level with the girl. "You need to speak slowly, okay? Tell me. What happened?"

"He locked me in the closet!"

"Who locked you in the closet?"

Elsie scanned the faces around her. It was a matter of time before she looked up. This was Jack's house. There was nowhere for him to go.

"Elsie?" The tone of her mother's voice had edged into panic, and the atmosphere in the room shifted. "*Who* are you talking about?"

Jack would not remember exactly when all the eyes set upon them. It must have happened little by little, then all at once. It was not Elsie who noticed them first, but his mother. Jack had not even seen her in the throng of parents.

She was holding a bottle opener. The night had taken a toll on her, her eyelids heavy and swollen. In the light, her makeup appeared caked on, as if he could make out each layer. She met his eyes, or his father's, he couldn't tell.

Then all the guests at the party were looking at him, or his father—he still couldn't tell. The longer they looked, the more it seemed to him that they were not simply acknowledging the presence of father and son. They were deciding between them.

Who are you talking about?

Who touched you? Who is he?

What happened next couldn't have lasted more than a few seconds. When a question so electric hangs in the air, a few seconds is all one needs to seize on an answer. Annabel, feeling the weight of the faces, no longer wishing perhaps to be in the spotlight, turned away from the eyes, turned not toward her father but to her brother. She buried her face in Jack's chest. One month ago he'd found her sleepwalking in the kitchen, and he'd let that swinging door crash into her head. This time, he picked her up and carried her the rest of the way down the stairs, his arms firm and strong.

Jack's descent created a separation between him and his father. It could not have been more than a few feet, but the eyes of the spectators widened the rift. They trained on his father, making calculations. Even his mother looked at Liang that way.

"Liang, what's going on here?" said Elsie's father. His voice was hoarse. "Help me understand. Help me out here. Please."

His father coughed. He said, "You don't understand—"

"No, damn it, we *don't* understand," said Elsie's mother.

"Melissa," Jack's mother attempted, but Elsie's mother shushed her.

"It probably comes as no surprise to you that we had major reservations coming here," she said, shooting another sharp look at her husband. "I tried to be generous. God knows the teachers certainly have been. So I thought maybe, *maybe* this abuse my daughter was receiving from your daughter was all a misunderstanding. Now I'm beginning to wonder if I've misunderstood something else altogether."

Annabel was crying again. Jack brought her closer, her body a plank in his arms, and cooed reassurances to her.

"Jack?" His father's voice again. His father, calling out to him. "Jack? You were there . . . yes? Tell them I didn't do this. Annabel was . . . she was . . . Jack, they were playing game, yes? Tell them they were playing game."

Jack could not move his face away from his sister's, could not face his father, not now, could not bear to see the eyes that had surely turned to him. There was nothing good to come from being seen. Better to keep his cheek pressed against his sister's.

His father was still calling to him. "Jack? Érzi, gàosu tāmen."

But Jack could not tell them. He could only hold on to this smaller body until that body softened, and he softened, and they melted.

"Érzi?" his father tried again.

This time, it was Elsie's father who came to Jack's rescue. "Wasn't he hiding?"

Jack peered up, quickly enough to meet the man's eyes.

"I mean, they were playing hide-and-seek," Elsie's father went on. "Jack, buddy. Did you see what happened? You can talk to me. We just want to sort this out."

If Jack said what his father wanted him to say, who would be punished? The eyes that now looked at him, Annabel's protector, with compassion, even admiration, would turn back to daggers of accusation. *You said you were going to watch them*, they'd say. *You promised*. And his sister . . . who knew? At best, she'd become a pariah at her school, like Marco Martinez. At worst, she would be arrested—sent wherever Naveen Naidu had gone. There were such things as jails for kids. Elsie's father had said as much.

It would take only a few hours for Jack to shoot down his own reasoning, to ask himself why he'd said what he'd said, and why he had not thought about the consequences that would lie in store for his father. But in that moment, with all the adults waiting for him to speak, he believed that when someone like Elsie's father asks you a question, you answer.

"I wasn't there," he said.

The commotion that followed drowned out his own thoughts. Questions were fired into the air. Side conversations led to louder pronouncements led to yelling. Elsie's parents both yelled. Jack could not hear himself rethinking his lie, imagining alternate scenarios. He had said what he'd said, and to walk back his words now would be a greater crime than uttering them.

As for Jack's father, he said only, "I saw you, Jack—at the door, you were—" He sounded as if he were trying to pull words out of mud. "Annabel, tell them . . ."

Then Jack's mother: "He said he was not there."

She had tried to say it softly enough so only Jack's father

could hear, but Jack still made it out. It was one thing to tell a lie, another thing for your mother to believe you. He was her jīn gǒu, wasn't he? He was gold, golden, goldest. And as her belief in Jack's words spread through her to everyone around her, Jack was not sure that he could even call what he'd said a lie. Yes, he had stood outside Annabel's bedroom and watched what had happened. But what had happened, anyway? When you look straight at the sun, you don't see the sun so much as the sky around it. His father had told him that.

Annabel clung to Jack. She refused to face the commotion around her. So let her miss it, Jack thought. Let her fall asleep right now in his arms. He was doing what he was supposed to do. He was here now, he told his sister. He was here.

6

On her first day back to work from maternity leave, Patty had woken up thinking that something horrible was going to happen. She had carried that thought through a quiet breakfast with her family, a surprisingly light commute downtown, all the way to her cubicle, which she then discovered had been lent to an intern—an intern who appeared, at different times in the day, to be two different interns, though she was too embarrassed to ask. Her coworkers' conversations hovered out of reach somehow, and when Patty attempted to join in on a subject other than Annabel, she sensed that she was intruding, as if they'd all been talking about her. Much had changed in her absence. There had been a hushed round of layoffs in corporate comms.

Rumors of a merger with a company based out of Vienna. On the drive home, a stretch she'd recalled as blocked off by construction for the foreseeable future had been replaced by clean, suspiciously slippery concrete.

Feeling disoriented, she switched lanes after getting off 75 without checking her blind spot, causing a man in a silver Corolla to honk at her for a good minute. She would not remember what he looked like, only that he'd stared at her, or rather the back of her, with a hatred that reminded her of faces on the news—that woman whose husband had been falsely imprisoned for murder, that man whose daughter had died from an IED. When she changed lanes again, the Corolla changed too, and when she changed back, the Corolla followed suit. Sometimes a car got between them, but the Corolla always reappeared in her rearview mirror. The driver took her exit, then the same turn, then another. It wasn't until he entered Huntington Villa behind her that the possibility of his following her seized at Patty. Her fingers locked around the steering wheel. It was dark by then. She could no longer make out the man's face. Maybe he was a parent like her, coming home to his spouse and children. Maybe he was one of her neighbors. She had met only four or five of them.

It occurred to her that she could drive past Plimpton Court, take Main Street all the way out of the community, perhaps straight to the nearest police station. But to do so would be to succumb—even in the privacy of her own mind—to the conviction that the awful feeling she'd had returning to work had somehow led to this. That she could actually think horrible events into existence. Was that not a reality crazier than some driver with a case of road rage? Annabel's birth had gone so according to plan that Patty had been sure something was wrong. Those were the first words she'd said upon meeting her new baby: *Something is wrong.* Liang had looked at Patty the same way her boss had looked at her upon her return, when, first thing in the morning, she'd requested months-old updates. Liang turned away from her worry, made her turn away with him. He kissed her everywhere. Kissed the wisps of the baby's hair, already full and black.

Qīng-Qīng, please—

No. Something is wrong.

No, thought Patty as she turned onto her street that night. Everything had been fine. Easing off the pedal in front of her home, she did not allow herself to think that she was leading a potential murderer to her family. The Corolla slowed down at the intersection, idling long enough to give the driver time to catch her car turning in to her driveway—and then he moved on. She never saw him again, as far as she knew.

Now, the morning after the Thanksgiving party, Patty woke up feeling the same way. That ridiculous, nagging fear. For the first time in years, she recalled that drive home, hunched close to the wheel with the headlights of the Corolla behind her. Her back ached now as it had then. She sat up in bed and looked around. The air felt disturbed, as if a stranger had swept through and, touching nothing, left.

Across Plimpton Court, another mother—Zoe Martinez, by the sound of her voice—was hurrying her family inside their car. "Chop-chop," she kept saying. A door slid closed and the car drove off, returning the street to its sleepy state. Patty's hands still smelled of dish soap, her fingers stained from dumping full glasses of wine into the sink. Next to her, Annabel slept on her side, legs and arms frozen in the pose of a runner.

Liang was gone. He'd left a sticky note on the nightstand: *Shopping.*

Patty got up to check the dresser mirror, half expecting to see herself the way she'd looked pulling into the garage after the scare with the Corolla, the door taking excruciatingly long to roll down behind her. But the face in the mirror now did not look alarmed, only tired.

She picked up Liang's note, inspected the scrawl of letters. If anything was wrong, it was this. They hadn't braved the Black Friday crowds for years. They didn't need anything. As she wandered out of the bedroom, she thought of picking up the phone to check on Liang, before stopping herself. Maybe what he needed was to be alone.

They had barely spoken since the party last night. After

the other guests sheepishly followed the Louise-Deflieses out the front door, Liang took Annabel to bed, leaving Patty to do the dishes. He did not explain himself. He did not explain, Patty reminded herself now, because there was nothing to explain. A dǎodànguǐ like Elsie spewed nonsense. When Patty had joined him in bed, she'd muttered an apology for inviting the girl's parents, but Liang had fallen asleep.

She would apologize again when he came back. *No problem, I will handle,* as Raj, Karl, Chethan, and Pranav would say. Concentrate: one Fruit Loop after another. By the time Patty finished her cereal, the children had joined her at the kitchen table. She poured them more Fruit Loops. Jack watched the rings grow soggy, while Annabel scarfed hers down. How strange to be home on a Friday morning, even if the office was closed. When Annabel asked about Daddy, Patty said that he was getting their Christmas gifts. Jack excused himself with half his cereal floating in his bowl. She had an urge to call after him, to tell him not to worry. Why did he look so worried?

Annabel was asking another question.

"Māma, what does *abducted* mean?"

Patty could tell her, *abducted means eating a duck.* She could tell her, *I abducted you from your real mother.* Annabel did not ask questions to discover the truth, she asked because she wanted to know that there was someone who could answer in such a way that made her feel safe, made her feel less alone and confused.

SIMON HAN

Patty was not that someone, not this morning. "No more. Not now."

"But—"

"Háizi. Māma is tired."

"Because of the party?"

"Yes. Because of the party."

Annabel shot up from her seat. "Later, can I go to Elsie's?"

"Did you hear me?"

Annabel would not accept it. Not to be able to ask a question! It went against every teaching in the Plano Star Care handbook. The same handbook that had probably taught Annabel the word *abducted* along with Elsie's nonsense. Perhaps the solution to the Elsie problem was to remove Annabel from that school. What did it matter that she'd finally gotten accepted, after two failed tries? Jack hadn't gone to private school, and he'd turned out fine—better, even. "Annabel, I'm serious. I need quiet."

The girl kept fussing. She rattled her spoon against the bowl. She crouched with all four limbs on her chair, as if she intended to lunge, pantherlike, across the table. She refused to bring her leftovers to the sink as Patty had been teaching her to do. Then she picked up a single Fruit Loop, hand dripping with milk, and flicked it.

Slowly, Patty plucked the Fruit Loop out of her hair. Deposited it on the table. Watching her daughter across the table,

168

the little peaks of her shoulders rising to match the arcing of her brows—a strained attempt at villainy—Patty wondered if maybe she had gotten the girl wrong. What if Annabel was the kind of child who deserved a slap in the face? She let herself imagine it, reaching over and, without holding back, delivering a blow that would knock the girl, and her chair, to the ground. Patty had never hit her children. What she felt, imagining it, was not unlike what she'd felt after that garage door had closed behind her that night, shutting out the silver Corolla. Relief. Yes. But regret overcame her just as quickly. Annabel watched her as if she could read her mind. *Don't look at me like that*, Patty thought. *It was a passing—*

The doorbell rang.

She joined Annabel in a sprint to welcome Liang back, only to find a stranger there.

Her name was Marcy Thomas, and on the business card she would leave Patty, a card that Patty would read and reread every day for the next month, turning the thin stock to the light as if a different, secret message might appear, her official title was Investigator Specialist. She was a Black woman, over a foot shorter than Patty and just taller than Jack. Her beige trench coat draped down to her ankles. The picture on her badge looked like someone who could be Marcy's daughter, or niece. Marcy did not look old so much as experienced, as if she'd been doing this job for a long time, even on holidays.

"No need to take my coat," she told Patty. "Nice to meet you, darling," she said to Annabel, introducing herself to the girl as Miss Marcy and bending down to shake her hand. Patty was not sure if she had ever seen her daughter shake a stranger's hand. Marcy Thomas was with the Department of Family and Protective Services, she explained. She was following up on a report, there was no need to worry, no need at all. This was a *routine house visit*, she said.

"Were you invited?" Annabel asked.

Marcy smiled. "Well, in a way."

"You can't *visit* if you weren't *invited*."

"Háizi." Patty dragged Annabel toward her, a gesture that Marcy seemed to take special interest in. The woman suggested they go for a walk inside, as if Patty's home was a stroll around the block.

"The party was *yesterday*," Annabel said, and Patty, without changing her expression, responded in Mandarin that if she kept interrupting, she would be sent to the closet.

"It's not really my place to ask this," Marcy said, "but would you mind speaking only in English? For now? Again, I know it's not my place."

Patty licked the roof of her mouth. "Of course," she said. "I'm sorry."

"No need to apologize. It would help to move things along, that's all. *I'm* sorry to have to intrude on your family's Thanksgiving. Speaking of which, your husband . . ."

"I will call him. He should be back soon."

Liang did not answer his phone, as Patty followed the woman around the house. Cups and balled-up napkins still littered the piano room. In the living room, there was a stain on the rug that was either wine or blood—Patty hadn't noticed until Marcy did. Marcy opened drawers and cabinets, peered into the refrigerator. Turned the milk carton around, checking the expiration date. At least Patty had done the dishes.

She tried Liang a few more times. "So sorry," she told Marcy. "The timing is very bad. My husband wishes to be here, maybe store is too busy."

Marcy said, "I would really prefer not to have to come back."

"Oh, yes. Me, too." Patty held back a wince. She dragged forward the leg Annabel was clinging to. What *do* you say to an uninvited visitor? The questions Patty wanted to ask—*Why are you here? What will you do? Are you going to take my children?*—she pushed back. In their place: "Water? Tea? Coffee? How about blueberry pie? One of our guests brought it last night, but no time to eat. Good bakery! Not some Kroger quality."

"If you don't mind, Mrs. Cheng, I'd like to just move things along."

Upstairs, the woman met Jack, hiding out in the home office. This was her jīn gǒu, Patty said to Marcy. "Sorry, I used Chinese again. It means 'gold dog.' In China, calling your child a dog is not a bad thing."

It seemed every time Patty spoke, all Marcy had to offer in return was a simple *Mm-hmm*. A *Yes*. A *Wonderful*. They all sounded the same, from her mouth.

"Did you have a good Thanksgiving?" Marcy asked Jack, who nodded. Unlike Annabel, the boy did not ask questions. He watched Marcy watch him. There was no way to get out of Marcy's crosshairs. She seemed to have the power to look at his big toe and make it wiggle. Something about the woman in her house made Patty feel like the visitor, as if she could not step between her and Jack until Marcy told her she could.

"Jack does not sleep enough," Patty offered. "He is *usually* very good, of course. Not many problems with him, this child. That is not saying Annabel has problems. She is lucky to have a big brother like him. Eleven years old! I cannot really complain. At least, I tell him to sleep more. Do you hear that, Jack? Mom knows best, right?"

Marcy sat down on the sofa in the office. "If it's all right with you, I'd like to focus on the children." From the deep pockets of her trench coat, she removed a silver recorder—slightly bigger than the PEZ candy dispensers that Jack used to collect.

How was their day? Marcy asked the children. Any fun plans for the weekend? It was okay if she recorded them, right? Listening to her questions, Patty wondered if they were excuses for her to keep staring. Was Marcy trying to find a bruise? And why did Patty feel nervous, when she had nothing to hide? Marcy asked the children about their favorite foods. She asked them how often they got to eat their favorite foods. And what about their favorite drinks? How often did they get to drink their favorite drinks?

"And your dad? Does he have a favorite drink?"

"Ma'am," Patty said, "I do not understand—"

"Mrs. Cheng—"

"I do not understand the point of these questions."

"As I told you, it's just procedure."

"It's okay, Mom." There was Jack again. She did not need to tell him how to act, what to say. Water, he replied. Tea. Coffee. His dad was like any other dad. Meanwhile, Annabel climbed onto the sofa with Patty, forced her way into her lap. Whenever she had an audience, she was eager to perform. Today, she was playing a daughter who deserved to be slapped.

"You *said* Daddy's coming back. Where is he?"

SIMON HAN

Patty tried to rein her in with a firm grip. The recorder was recording, and Marcy was watching. Maybe she could read Patty's mind, too. She tried to think about something else, anything else, but when she cleared her head, all she could see was Elsie running down the stairs. The horror on the little girl's face. What she'd said, what she'd claimed Liang had done. It was easier to imagine Elsie lying. Yes, it was easier.

At last, Marcy looked away. She'd exhausted all her questions. She suggested that they check out the children's rooms, and the two left the children behind, with brother roping sister into a game of Connect Four.

Relieved as Patty was not to have to deal with Annabel for the moment, it was more frightening to be left alone with Marcy Thomas. She felt as if the woman were some kind of detective. In Jack's room, the pillow was propped against the bed frame. There was an open book at his desk, open blinds looking out to Plimpton Court, and an open closet door, populated with a few empty hangers, a couple of them curiously swinging in place. Then they moved on to Annabel's room, and Patty explained that all the nightlights served as outlet plugs on top of helping her daughter sleep. "Wonderful," Marcy said. She jiggled Annabel's doorknob, which like Jack's did not have a lock. She peered out the window that overlooked the neighbor's backyard. She glanced at the full-length mirror. She looked closer. "What's this?" she said, pointing at the corner of the mirror.

There was a thin crack, the size of one of Annabel's fists. At first Patty had thought it was a spider web. When she pressed against the crack on the glass, it grew.

"You might not want to touch that," Marcy said.

"I've never seen this before."

"Your daughter's quite the ball of energy. Maybe it was an accident?"

Patty did not mention that, these days, Annabel almost never played in her bedroom. She almost never went upstairs at all. That was, aside from last night.

"Yes," she said. "An accident."

A pause. "Yes?"

"I don't know what they told you."

"Mrs. Cheng. What was an accident?"

Patty tried to smile. Then she laughed. "An accident? No, no, nothing. No one did any kind of bad thing, not in this house. This house is a safe place. My children are happy."

"Well, of course. This is what we both want. But if there's any helpful context that you may be in a position to offer . . ."

Patty cut in: "I don't know about the glass, but I will fix. This I can fix."

After a few more sweeping looks and an outlining of procedural details, Marcy announced that it was time for her to go. Liang still had not returned Patty's call, and there was nothing more Marcy could do for the moment. She would be in touch, she said. Patty and the children walked her to the front door. The woman shook both children's hands before she stepped out. Together, they watched her take a lifetime looping around the cul-de-sac in her gray van. After Patty went back inside, she closed the door and leaned against it. *Concentrate*, she thought. *Disappear.* When she opened her eyes, her children were still standing before her.

"Mom?" Jack said. He kept looking at the closed door behind her, as if Marcy Thomas might come barging back. "Did I mess up, Mom?" He seemed on the verge of tears. Patty had missed the years when he cried. If he cried now, it would be like watching a grown man cry. She could no longer run his sadness through a cost-benefit analysis the way she sometimes did with Annabel's fits, or distressing news on TV. How long would the sadness last? How much of an empathetic investment did it warrant? What was the fastest route to a short-term or long-term solution?

Surprising herself, she brought her son closer, hugged him. "No, not at all. No, you didn't, my jīn gǒu'r." Eventually the edges of his body softened. His arms, almost as long as hers now, made their way around her back. His hands landed on her so lightly she did not know that she had been touched. "Hey, what if I warm some pie, hǎobuhǎo?"

Around the kitchen island, the three of them ate without talking. Annabel was too short to see over the counter, but she refused to let anyone pick her up or move the pie to the table. She reached blindly above her and Jack guided her fork into the crust. Patty rolled warm blueberries over and under her tongue. She did not mention anything about lunch, and the children did not ask. The pie was sweet and ample enough. They were a family that enjoyed their pie. That was all they needed to be. They kept eating as the filling turned cold.

"If only she saw us like this," Patty said.

But as Patty watched Jack help his sister to another bite, she thought no, no. Better a stranger not see them like this. Better not to give a single detail away. Only after the pie was done and Jack had gone upstairs did she take Annabel into her lap and ask her, while braiding the girl's hair, the question that had been gnawing at her since last night.

"Bǎobèi. Daddy didn't give Elsie a bad touch actually, right? Can you tell me what happened?"

Annabel shook her head.

"You mean, nothing happened, or you can't tell me?"

She shook her head again. "Not Elsie. Daddy gave a bad touch to me."

. . .

Bad touch. Was there a more disturbing pair of words? They meant one thing on their own, another thing joined together, and Annabel—thank god—did not seem to grasp the difference. Last night, the girl went on to explain, the way one tried to narrate a dream, the story of the dream becoming more solid than the dream itself—last night, Daddy had gotten mad at her, had shoved her against the mirror, and it had hurt. It had really hurt. Was that a bad touch? Did that count?

That's all? Patty asked, as if a story of her husband shoving their daughter into a mirror so hard it had cracked could be a relief, but it was, she had to admit that it was, though she still could not fill in the gaps. There were moments, even in waking life, when it seemed Liang did not know the pain that he could inadvertently cause another person—a too-tight squeeze of his hands, a too-sudden turn of his wrist. What had angered him in the first place?

Annabel blamed Elsie. Elsie had been her Elsie self, hurling pillows across the room, knocking down Māma's flowers and making a mess and all of that had made Annabel, well, *excited*; they had been so excited to play outside of school, but then Annabel suddenly went quiet. Was she in trouble? she asked Patty. Could she still play with Elsie?

"Of course not," Patty said, which the girl assumed was an

answer only to the first question. Annabel's braided hair un-knotted, fell over her back. *A fierce spirit,* Mrs. King had said during an early parent-teacher conference. *With a natural cha-risma that we don't even see in our, well, presidents.* Patty pulled her closer in her lap. "Tell me, bǎobèi. You can trust me." But Annabel had moved on. She was yawning. She was tired, she said, even as her body remained stiff, a thing that adults did when they lied.

Liang came home in the late afternoon, bearing gifts, just as Patty had claimed earlier that morning. Could she call what she'd told the children a lie if it turned out to be true? Light-up sneakers and Bratz dolls spilled out of their boxes, which spilled out of their bags. He didn't bother to sneak the gifts into the closet, where they could sit until Christmas. Why wait? said Liang, a sentiment to which Annabel emphatically agreed. Father and daughter sat cross-legged on the floor, mak-ing a mess of cardboard and plastic and shopping-bag tissue paper.

He did not know what had happened, Patty understood then. His phone had died early in the morning, so he hadn't even known she'd called fourteen times. For the time being, whatever silences had sat between them since last night would keep on living; she was grateful for them. After Annabel's pres-ents, Liang ducked in and out of the garage, bringing back larger bags and boxes. A red bow. A wreath. Extension cords.

Stringed lights. Webbed lights. Ribbons, garlands, pinecones. Ornaments—two already smashed. A tree. Yes, he had purchased a tree in a box.

She did not know when to bring up the CPS visit. She did not know how to say, *There's a woman who has the power to take away our children.* She had spent the afternoon doing research online, had found contact information for a few good lawyers, but with Liang before her she did not know where to begin. Marcy Thomas's business card sat in the back pocket of Patty's jeans, as obtrusive in her mind as a knife. Liang was too busy playing Santa Claus in November to notice. He called to Jack. The boy was slow to come down the stairs, slower to accept the gift. "Go on," Liang said, presenting the most impressive box of the haul. "It's not a bomb." It was a Razor scooter.

Jack muttered a thanks. As he sat down to cautiously inspect the scooter, Annabel planted one of her Bratz dolls on her father's shoulder. Patty could almost hear the oversize plastic high heels clicking. Annabel leaned the doll's head toward Liang's ear, the body-length straw-blond hair tickling his neck. The doll was whispering to him.

"Daddy, an intruder came to our house today."

Of course Annabel would be the one to tell him. Well, let her go on—Patty was too tired to delay any longer. It was Jack who rushed over and snatched up the doll, as if the doll were the culprit. Did Jack know what Marcy Thomas could do? If he hadn't looked so serious, Liang might have thought Anna-bel was playing another game.

At first, Liang looked more curious than angry. He glanced at Patty for confirmation. "Ah, it was Helen, yes? She forgot her scarf?"

"Liang." It was Patty's turn now. She wished there was a language they could speak that her children could not under-stand. "Can we go to the bedroom?"

"She was looking for *you*," Annabel said.

"Annabel—"

"*You're* in *trouble*, Daddy."

"Stop it," Patty said.

It took another minute for the details to be coaxed out. Finally, Patty showed him the business card. There had been a time when Liang had business cards, when he'd handed them out to strangers. She wanted to tell him that the CPS visit was all a mistake, a misunderstanding. She watched him instead.

Liang was a handsome man; she had always thought so. He had a belly she liked, and wide, strong hips. The wrinkles on his face appeared only when he smiled. He looked as if he'd always had a good night's sleep, even when he hadn't—and even now, after a full day of shopping. This gave his anger a theatrical air. If she distanced herself enough from the sight, she could convince herself that he was an actor from a glitzy

Broadway musical, playing an irate man from the Shaanxi countryside.

Then his voice came back to her, louder. "What did you tell her?" He said it with accusation, and this angered her in turn. "Patty. Answer me."

"Is there something I *should* tell her?"

She knew she'd misspoken, but she didn't care. It wasn't the children Liang seemed worried about. He had barked her English name with the coldness of a dissatisfied customer. "What did *he* tell her?" he said, meaning Jack, not even deigning to call him by name.

His finger stabbed the air in Jack's direction, again and again, but he did not touch the boy. Patty felt queasy. Jack's face blanched. Though they were all only a few feet from one another, she could see Liang the way Jack was seeing him. The finger. The blurry body. She wrapped Liang with her arms from behind. There had been a time when she'd greeted him that way. Now she let go, turning him to face her, steering him away from Jack.

"Let's go for a drive," she said. She did not like the idea of leaving her children alone in the house, considering someone from CPS could return at any moment. What would be worse—for Marcy to see them alone, or for Marcy to see Liang like this? *Chéng Liàng*, she pleaded, *Chéng Liàng*. She had been in the house all day and could use some fresh air. Jack could watch his sister for ten or so minutes, couldn't he?

Liang relented. He followed Patty to the garage, though not without grumbling something to himself that she was glad she could not hear. Behind them, Jack sat with his sister among the piles of gifts, no words passing between them.

"Man of the house," she said to Jack in English, with a tired wink. "I know you'll be good."

The temperature outside was the same as it had been inside. The air felt recycled, as if she were stepping out of a store and into a mall, from one contained space to a larger contained space. Inside this outside, the sun had come down. Patty had barely enough time to zip up her boots before Liang claimed the driver's side of his Volvo. Once they were both seated, he peeled out of the driveway.

There was no rush, she told him. There was nowhere they needed to be. The magnanimous Santa Claus version of her husband had disappeared within minutes, replaced with a man on a mission. She did not know his mission, but he roiled against an invisible force to accomplish it. He turned out of their community without braking. He nearly ran over a traffic

SIMON HAN

cone. Patty thought she saw a police car; when she mentioned it to Liang he said that she hadn't. Only when she put a hand on his arm did he ease up on the accelerator.

As he veered onto Legacy, Patty tried to explain the situation. She treaded lightly, going over the most basic details. At every turn, she emphasized what she'd read online: that in a city like theirs, in a neighborhood like theirs, children from a family like theirs simply did not get taken away. Liang would have to call this Marcy to schedule an interview, she said. He had to only because he hadn't been at home when she came. It wasn't as if Liang was a *suspect*. She stopped herself. What was she doing, talking about suspects?

Liang responded with as few words as Marcy Thomas had. It no longer comforted Patty to know that he did not feel the need to explain himself. She felt that he needed to explain himself. A voice warbled from the radio she hadn't realized was on: *WARNING: Studies predict texting while driving will become the leading cause of vehicular accidents and deaths . . .*

Liang braked too hard, accelerated too fast. It wasn't clear if he was listening to her or the radio. *So if you want twenty-twenty vision and you want it now, pull over to the side of the road before texting S-E-E to reserve your free consultation with Dr. Kensok . . .*

At last, they came to a stop. There was a rare pedestrian crossing outside the Shops at Legacy. Revelers were filing out of the bars and clustering outside, most of them around the

184

age Patty and Liang had been when they'd come to America. Some had surely grown up here, come home for the holidays to visit their parents. They were dressed as if they were going to work, though arms slid into crooks, hands slid down backs.

"You must be tired," she said.

Liang pressed his lips together. "These days, it is more tiring to sleep."

His voice sounded calmer, finally eased up. She pictured him walking around the Galleria earlier in the day, accumulating so many gifts he'd had to pack them into one of those two-seated fire-truck-themed strollers. Maybe he'd paused to gaze at the giant Christmas tree and the ice skaters that swarmed around it—ten thousand ornaments and half a million LED lights, all two thousand branches meticulously sculpted so not a single one stuck out.

Now he drove on, leaving the gold-laced lights of the Shops blinking behind them. The empty roads that cut through the JCPenney and Frito-Lay office parks gave the night a hollowed-out feeling, as if they were driving through an abandoned parking garage. Patty found herself talking not about the CPS visit, or the mall, but about the night six years ago when the man in the silver Corolla had followed her home.

That night, when she'd finally stepped inside the house, her family was waiting at the kitchen table. Liang had prepared an elaborate spread to celebrate her return to work.

From the door, she could smell her favorite sea bass, the ginger and soy sauce. She could identify every dish—the shrimp and snow peas, the steamed eggs, the pickled cucumber—and the hands that had made them. Annabel was there, too, perched in her rocker by Jack's dangling feet. Jack met his mother's eyes instead of directing them to a book or a Game Boy. She smiled back her fear and sat down with them. Before she could pick up her chopsticks, Liang reached for her hand, holding it in his own, as if in prayer. That was when Patty decided not to tell him.

"I didn't want to ruin my memory of that night," she said.

Liang's hand slid down from the wheel. "So this man," he said to the road, "in the silver Corolla. He saw you turn into our house. The eighth house from Main Street."

"Yes, but he could have been anyone."

"Yes, Qīng-Qīng. Anyone."

His eyes were still aimed a hundred miles down the road. What was he thinking? Perhaps he thought her selfish to put her family in danger like that. What if the man had come back? What if he had been waiting six years, and came back now?

Liang continued looking straight. She said, "Let's go back."

He did not move his head. "Where?"

"What do you mean?" she said.

Liang made a U-turn, and headed east on Legacy. He was

driving steadily now, in the direction of home. Hedgcoxe. Preston. Coit. Liang named the streets they passed, the same streets they'd always passed. Patty felt as if she were in one of their early home videos. It had been years since she'd watched one of them. "Who do you think these streets are named after?" Liang said. "Are they real people? Did they walk these streets before?"

"I don't know," she said. "I just know the names."

He pointed at a fire hydrant. "Why is it red in Annabel's picture books, but blue and silver here?" He aimed his chin at a grassy median. "What was there before that ugly grass? What should we call those weeds?"

"A weed is a weed," she said. They were almost back.

"No," Liang said. "It's not."

Patty gently squeezed his arm. "You missed the turn."

Liang continued driving. His eyes were fixed forward. Not Huntington Villa. Not home.

She said, "Where are we going?"

Maybe he was looking at the moon. *Lift my head and see the moon, lower my head and miss my home*: a line from a Lǐ Bái poem, the one with which he'd surprised her on a night early in their marriage. Some sleepless nights, he'd speak to the moon outside their bedroom. He'd speak of the quiet grace of his mother, how she'd died in an accident when he was young; of his father, who'd left him to live in the mountains with other men; of his Qīng-Qīng, who would one day be a mother, though at that point they had not once made love.

"Here we are, Qīng-Qīng."

She surveyed the Taco Bell, the Starbucks, the Chase Bank. There was another tutoring academy, another orthodontist's office. "What are you talking about? Where?" She looked at the clock, and it dawned on her how she'd made her children skip lunch, how hungry they might be. "The children."

He bowed his head. "My children are in good schools, my wife has a good job. My house is nice, my neighborhood nice. All nice, you say. CPS is understaffed, overwhelmed. We will get through this, you say. I am not so sure."

"Liang. Please."

They were about to reach Montmartre, the neighborhood where Helen and Jerry and their college dropout daughter, Charlene, lived, where a week ago she'd had to shuttle Liang over in the morning to pick up the car he'd been too drunk to drive the night before. It was here that he eased up on the pedal.

One day after Thanksgiving, the famed lights of Montmartre were already in bloom. Liang drove past the reds and greens and blues, the elegant houses with all silver. Light pulsed down from Bradford pears like raindrops. Nativity scenes came in all shapes, sizes, species. From one lawn, a chorus of bundled-up carolers rotated in a perpetual circle, singing Christmas classics channeled from an AM station.

I used to have legs, the radio said, from a different station, *before I did drugs.*

The lights grew brighter as they approached the Huangs' street. But Liang passed that turn as well. "Please," Patty said. If he registered the uneasiness on her face, he no longer seemed to care. He glanced left and right, while she scanned the inside of the car, lingering on the red switch by the handle. The door was locked. Of course it was. If she reached over and unlocked it, would Liang notice?

There was not much time to let her mind wander. Finally, Liang brought the Volvo to a halt. He'd parked in front of a house unlike any they'd yet seen. Massive floodlights from the edge of the lawn cast its two stories in high definition. Against the backdrop of light, thousands of snowflakes—or rather, the intricate shadows of snowflakes, danced and twirled. On the lawn, human-size screens displayed loops of familiar silhouettes, from a herd of flying reindeer to a boy and girl kissing under mistletoe.

Liang did not have any interest in the light show. "Forgive me," he said, his voice cracking. "For a second, I'd thought you were the one who had called CPS."

Patty sat still. No, she had not reported her own husband.

She had still not asked him about last night, either. How strange. She had not given much thought to who had reported them.

Then it came to her. "Elsie's parents. They live here, too."

Later, she would wonder what had set Liang off in the end. Was it seeing where they lived? Was it how much bigger and nicer the house was than their own? Or was it the way she'd looked at him, while they were parked outside? Her eyes betraying a thought that had settled in a corner of her mind, a thought that she had spent the past day trying to correct. What if. What if. What if Liang *had* done something terrible.

He turned away. "Jerry was telling me about this house. He was even thinking of inviting Elsie's dad to the next poker night. Can you believe it?"

"You don't have to go," Patty said.

"To poker night? Oh, I am done with that shit."

She followed his gaze to the house. The projections on the lawn had changed: a long arc of a shooting star spanned multiple screens.

"Jack," she said. "Annabel."

"As long as these people are here, our children are not safe," Liang said. "You were right, Qīng-Qīng. I should have done something. These parents, they are poisoning us. They are laughing behind our backs. They think they can point at a flower and call it a rock, and we will nod our heads."

"Let's go home. Let's discuss there." She took care to make her voice soft, steady.

"I *am* tired." Was he crying now? He was able to do it without a quiver in his body. He muttered something she couldn't decipher. After a minute, he quieted, hung his head like a child in trouble. "I'm sorry."

"We'll take Annabel out of school. It's all right."

"I'm sorry I did nothing." Liang said it this time in English, with the coldness of fact. His legs bobbed up and down, causing his voice to waver.

Again, Patty glanced at the red switch on her door. It wasn't as if she were going to run away, yet she couldn't help but look. She took her eyes off Liang for a second, and that was all the time he needed. The door opened and shut so fast he could have slipped through a crack of air. He crossed in front of the car toward the house. A Christmas tree blinked through one of the bay windows.

"Please," she called out to Liang from inside the car, but of course he could not hear. She held on to a fleeting hope that before he reached the door he would turn around, seek some sense, a talking back from the ledge.

Her husband went on, up the cobbled pathway. She knew then that she would not reach him. She would drive away instead of chasing after him. She could not be a part of whatever was going to happen. For her children's sake, she could not be a part of it. But even as her body shifted over to the driver's seat, as her hand moved toward the key still in the ignition, she kept watching. Against the white glare of the house's front door, Liang transformed into another shadow, bigger than the others, bigger than himself.

7

If Annabel was not moving herself, someone else was moving her. Huáng Āyí's daughter, Charlene, picked her up from her second new school in six months. A receptionist in a high-rise office led her to a small, windowless room while Māma talked to a suited man in a bigger room. One doctor sat her on top of a cushioned table and tapped her knee with a magic hand that sent her leg flying. Another doctor sat with her on a couch that made her want to sleep, and asked her about her highs and lows. Sometimes, to hurry her along, Māma draped her over one of her clothes-hanger shoulders. Now, on the other side of the car window, street signs whipped past them. Less than a full week into the New Year, she had perfected the trick of staying still and watching the world blur.

Since the day after Thanksgiving, Daddy had also never stopped moving. He'd been in such a rush that night that he had forgotten to pack a suitcase. First he drove his car to Los Angeles, Māma said, to fill in for a distinguished guest at a photography symposium. This made him, of course, a distinguished guest in his own right. He was so distinguished that he was then invited to China to receive an award, and though this meant he had to spend Christmas there, Māma said that he was thinking about her and Jack, buying them so many toys that by the time he came back Annabel would have enough gifts to last five Christmases.

And yet Annabel did not want anything from *China*. She said as much to Māma, who then scolded her for not appreciating where she came from. *She* hadn't come from China, Annabel said, though Māma had already moved on. During winter break, she was too busy sending Annabel to playdates or bringing Annabel and Jack to her office or transforming their house for Daddy's triumphant return. Garlands snaked around the upstairs bannister, and a plastic tree sprang from a mound of empty, already-opened boxes in the piano room. Four Christmas stockings, swelling with old Halloween candy, hung above the fireplace they never used. Māma even went outside in the cold, slinging lights around the bushes, over and under branches, saying bad words when they pricked her skin.

Meanwhile, Daddy still did not come back. On Christmas

Eve, Māma handed Annabel the phone, claiming the voice on the other end of the line belonged to him. *Bǎobèi*, the voice said. *Sorry we can't see the lights this year.* When Annabel asked the voice how it was possible to make phone calls from China, the voice talked instead of how wonderful it had been to visit the grandparents and great-uncles and aunts and cousins and second cousins whom Daddy had lost contact with after his mother went away. There were children there he'd never known, who before walking to school would plod down wheat fields and drop seeds in the holes that the adults in front of them had dug. The voice talked of the small pleasure of yams roasted over hot stones and dusted with wood ash. Those chilly evenings in the courtyard listening to Dàjiù's radio, the moon bright and full over the Qinling Mountains.

"No!" Annabel said. "I want pictures!" And when the voice told her that he no longer took photographs, that the teenagers who came to his studio were there for the white canvas, the fancy camera, and the dumb masks, she huffed and said that he wasn't making any sense. "Māma said you went to a picture-taking sym-pos-ee-um. Is Māma right?"

Immediately Māma jumped in. Daddy takes pictures for money, not fun. China is fun, not scary. Is Daddy no longer American? Oh, I don't know. Here, Liang. Talk to Jack. If the voice was Daddy's, why was Jack now quietly protesting? He looked at Māma as if to say *Not me, not me*, but Māma did not see what Annabel could see. When her brother finally accepted the phone, he stumbled over his words. *School is good grades are good friends good Mom good yes good yeah and Annabel is too. So.*

When the call ended, Annabel missed Daddy more than she had before. And though his absence grew bigger, each day he was gone eventually felt shorter. This, Annabel believed, was because time moved faster in 2004. There were resolutions to make, resolutions to fulfill. There were new children to impress, new stories with which to impress them. The truth about Santa was child's play; at Logan Elementary School, she pressed her ear to the playground pebbles and taught her classmates about China.

"Can you hear them?" she said, as a rapt circle formed around her. "Can you hear them screaming down there?"

A pale girl with a mop of brown hair gave it a try. "What are they saying?"

Annabel shoved her aside. *"I'm coming."*

What she didn't tell the others was that under the pebbles, the cracked clay, the earthworms and submerged ant colonies, her daddy's real voice mingled in chorus with the others. By then Annabel was sure that he'd been forced to stay in China, like the other Bad Guys. Whatever Bad Thing he'd done, she still believed Daddy would crawl his way back. That was another story she'd learned all her life: if you were not in America, you would do anything you could to get here. To the better place.

So she waited. And the days hurtled ahead. The monkey bars and musical chairs and you-are-special affirmations of Plano Star Care gave way to the dull picture books and unfenced playground of Logan Elementary School. Annabel accepted her new routine with the skepticism of one habituated to sudden and random disruptions. In the early mornings, Māma paced with her phone from stove to computer to the wreck of the kitchen table, speaking to India. She spoke in a different kind of English, using words like *test failure* and *production ramp delay*, with an authority she never showed to non-phone people. She penned messages onto her arms, pulling away when Annabel tried to read them. From afar, the words cast Māma in a sickly light, as if her skin were fading and the veins underneath turning a deeper blue. Every time Annabel asked her what she was doing, Māma would say, with resignation, *working*, which Annabel began to recognize as a bald-faced lie. What was happening, she suspected, was that Māma was *leaving*—that adult trick she'd perfected of remaining in a room while disappearing completely from it.

If Daddy was underground, Māma was in the clouds. She drifted about as if she were being carried away by her own receding voice. Whenever Annabel complained about her new school, Māma looked at her with exasperation. If her brother had gone to the same school and come out fine, why couldn't she? "It's still a great school. All you have to do is follow Gēge's example." She delivered commands that sounded more like statements, like an acceptance of their shared fate. Listen to your teachers. Speak well of your family. Show off your nice clean clothes. The tasty lunch I pack for you.

By the second week at Logan Elementary School, Annabel had taught her classmates all about Lee Harvey Oswald.

"After Lee Harvey Oswald died," she said, "he went to China."

A group of five other children crouched closer to Annabel on the sidewalk. Ian, a blond boy who wore Hawaiian shirts even in the winter, asked, "But what about John F. Candy?"

"Don't be dumb," Annabel said. "All presidents go to heaven."

The rest of the kindergarten class was melting ice cubes on the sidewalk so they could retrieve plastic spider rings encased in them. There was something they were supposed to learn from this, but the ice was taking too long to melt and the children around Annabel were far more interested in China. The grinding steel. The dragon-breath fires of eternal punishment. "Fascinating," they repeated after Annabel.

A taller girl named Jill Wu smashed her ice cube against the pavement. She said, "I like China."

Ian gasped. "But why?"

"I was born there," said Jill. "Yan was born there, too. And Walter!"

Annabel shook her head. "No way. You're just a baby."

"China's got a lot of babies. They got so much you can only have one each."

Annabel snickered. One baby? Then what would have happened if *she'd* been born in China? She was about to punt an insult back, but Jill had taken over.

"Sometimes, my mom cries in the car because she misses China so much. She used to tell Dad that we should go, but he always said money, money, money. Now she and Dad are separated, and she can go—and I'm going with her!"

Annabel's ears rang. "Separated?" she said.

"I'm so excited," Jill went on. "There's more stuff there."

"Yeah," said Annabel. "Lots of dirt."

"Mountains and rivers, and buildings as tall as mountains, and the tastiest food, and lots of money, and, and—" Jill beamed. "Happy stuff. More happy stuff."

Annabel's ice cube had nearly disappeared. She flung what little remained of it at Jill's stupidly proud face. The girl barely flinched; at best, Annabel had splashed her. Jill saw what her words were doing to Annabel, though, and made them louder:

"My mom's always saying, 'Why did I do this? Why did I leave my number one home for some last place man? Why? Why?' And you know what? My mom's *right*."

Annabel scowled. She wanted to shout, to use a scary adult word to get Jill to stop talking. But she was still hung up on *separated*. How was it that some words burrowed inside your ear and never left? When she'd told Elsie that scary story in her room to shut her up about Daddy, the words didn't fade away. Maybe Annabel had something to do with Daddy being in China; maybe she was not only Bad, but Worse.

Annabel stood up, staring down at the part in Jill's hair. She would pretend to be taller, like when Nice Daddy let her stand on the kitchen table. Like when she'd stood on the monkey bars at Plano Star Care. Like in that dream or maybe-dream, when she was outside, in the middle of the night, looking up at the bugs swarming around the moon. Though she could see her feet in the dream, she did not know how to make them move. And when they moved, she did not know how to make them stop. Maybe that was what it was like to walk on the moon.

Her teacher, Miss Katy, was calling for her. Annabel gave Jill one last glare and said, "You're such a Lee Harvey Oswald!" before marching off.

Miss Katy was standing by the door with a puzzled expression on her face. The lines around her jaw seemed on the verge of rupturing her bronzed skin. A woman in her midtwenties, her teacher took care of fifteen children by herself and pronounced Annabel's name like *in a bell*.

But as she led Annabel inside the school, Miss Katy did not say a thing. At the entrance to the kindergarten wing stood a woman in a pantsuit, a messenger bag slung over her shoulder. "Thank you," the visitor said. "Hey, Anna. Can I call you Anna? I like your shoes." Annabel recognized her face before her name. The roving eyes. The shiny hair and dark skin. Something had changed with Miss Marcy, too. Her voice was warm, almost milky. "I suppose we should go in here." The request sounded more like a consolation. The woman walked without hurry, trailing Annabel and her light-up sneakers to the kid chairs, the low and round tables flecked with Play-Doh, saliva, and other mysteries.

Why was the intruder here, at her new school of all places? Was it possible Māma had sent her? Annabel remembered what Māma had whispered to her in Chinese, when Miss Marcy wasn't paying attention: *Be good, like with your teachers. Do you want to get in trouble?* Miss Marcy, Annabel suspected, was less like a teacher and more like a Doctor Marcy or Officer Marcy.

"No more questions," Annabel said, and the woman laughed.

She said, "You really are your brother's sister."

They sat at the round table, not talking. Dapples of light and shadows from the sun and trees played lazily at their feet. Something was going to happen, Annabel thought.

"You know, I just saw Jack, before coming here," the woman said.

Annabel nodded, though this was news to her.

"Is it okay if I hang out with you, too? Just for a little while?"

A *no* was climbing up Annabel's throat, and she pushed it down. There was a comfort to Miss Marcy's honeyed smell, the shade of the curtains, the classmates playing outside, voices muffled as if they were far away. Even as Miss Marcy plucked from her bag the same rectangular silver gadget she'd used the time she'd visited their home, Annabel did not feel afraid. They were passing the time, as the adults would say.

"Thank you for being such a good helper." Miss Marcy's eyes lingered on Annabel. She seemed to be preparing for a long, arduous hike, only the room was nice and cool and they were not going anywhere. "Now I'm just going to speak into this thing here, like this. See?" Miss Marcy mimed words, and Annabel looked on. "Okay. Ready?"

There was a soundless tap of Miss Marcy's finger, and the red light on the silver block switched on. She cleared her throat. "Today is January twelfth, 2004. The time is, let's see, one thirteen p.m. My name is Marcy Thomas, CPS investigator, here at Logan Elementary School with . . . darling? Will you say your name for me, darling?"

• • •

A Problem Kid. That was what she became. By her third week at Logan Elementary, Annabel noticed the others moving in constant orbit around her, though not close enough to touch. From their poison stares to their sticky whispers, she patched together a scary story in which she played, at last, the starring role. Someone's parents had learned that Annabel Cheng was prone to using inappropriate words, saying shocking things; there had been a discussion with the teachers; children had been warned. Sentences began with *I know you might like her* and ended with *stay away*. Annabel was learning the nature of *but*.

Miss Marcy's visit hadn't helped, either. The day after their talk, everyone asked Annabel what she had gotten in trouble for. Annabel had not minded the visit, in the end. Yes, there had been strange questions: *Did she know the difference between a truth and a lie? Had anyone told her they were going to have this talk today? Where was she the day after Thanksgiving?* And yes, there had been a moment, as Annabel began her account of Daddy bringing home early Christmas presents, when Miss Marcy had opened her mouth to speak, only to slurp up the air, as if Annabel had flipped to the wrong page of her own story. But when they finished, the woman pressed a button on the silver gadget and the red light went off and she looked at Annabel with a tenderness Annabel hadn't felt for months and said, "They tell us not to do this. Can I give you a hug?" A hug Annabel remembered with bird-chirping fondness, a moment to keep for herself—not even Māma, who would be injured by its pleasantness, needed to know. Since the New Year, she and Māma had crossed some plane where Māma's pain was so constant, so neatly stitched, that neither of them seemed to register it.

"I heard you got kicked out of your old school," Jill said one afternoon. The two were sitting behind a partition in their classroom where the Legos and xylophones and dull picture books were shelved. On the other side, Miss Katy was supervising the rest of the children still struggling with their exercise sheets. The ones who finished early were using their library voices, which gave every word Annabel and Jill said the air of a secret.

"I got *transferred*," Annabel said. She wasn't sure what the word meant, but coming out of Māma's mouth, it had sounded like an accomplishment.

Jill smiled. "You're funny."

Annabel muttered a thanks, trying to make it sound sincere. How could someone in the same class as her understand so much more? It seemed Jill had become intimate with a part of Annabel that she had yet to discover herself.

"Everyone knows, Annabel."

Annabel shook her head. "What did I do?"

But Jill only smiled back.

"Hey, you. What did I do?"

Jill frowned. "You . . . you don't remember?"

How could Annabel remember? The past was not a thing that could be cobbled together from little parts. Unlike Māma's computer chips, it could not be pried open and laid out on a table. It seemed when the girl stepped into a room, the people inside had lived not only their entire lives, but years of hers as well. Before she was born, she was Annabel, the long-lost love of a poet from her parents' English textbook. She was a daughter, a sister, an American. She was, according to Daddy's words, *the luckiest*. Yet she was fragile before she knew that she could be broken. She was impressionable before she knew that she could be impressed. She was smaller than average before she knew what constituted an average. She had her mother's eyes and her father's nose before she knew the words *mother* and *father*.

Her first word, in English, was *whoa*.

Or was it *woe*?

The older Annabel got, the more adults poked their grubby fingers inside her brain. They accessed folds she had never entered herself. There was a reason she had trouble sleeping alone, they decided. Television was getting more violent, and so were her nightmares. She drew pictures of exploded heads because someone before her had drawn a picture of an exploded head.

Sometimes she slipped into a dream, one she'd be able to muscle into narrative only later in life. She is sitting between bookshelves in a musty library or the back room of some discount warehouse, rifling through the stacks. Each book has her face on the cover. She is reading a story a stranger has written about her life. She eventually settles on one book, turning the pages faster and faster until they're moving of their own volition, windblown and furious. In the dream, she can discern every word, each reeling toward a moment she will remember as one she desperately wishes not to arrive. *Don't*, she begins to say to herself, before she wakes up to her mother saying the same thing, fending off her kicks. *Don't—don't!*

Don't you remember? Maybe you're pretending.

Jack had said these words, that night when they'd run into each other in the upstairs hallway. Since the New Year, he'd stopped asking her about her sleepwalking, preferring to revisit memories that were real. If someone ever asked her about the Thanksgiving party, he said, she was to remember how her gēge had been hiding for most of the evening, playing the game that they'd wanted him to play. It seemed important to Jack that as his sister, she make him look good in front of the adults, so Annabel did not let him know how she'd already told Miss Marcy about Daddy being angry at Māma and Jack the night he left for Los Angeles. In front of her brother, it was a matter of acting. Annabel was good at acting, though acting like a sister was strange, and new.

In the rare times when Annabel went to Jack's room, she first knocked on his door and waited for his permission, as if she were a vampire. When she lay out on his bed, he rarely turned from his desk. He wrote in his books, even the library ones, words sprouting to the corners of the page. In a given moment, they could be sure of each other's presence only by remembering the last time they'd seen each other. Still, he was patient with her when she spoke.

"Am I a bad person?" she asked, one night in his room.

Jack set down his pen, looking down. "No, you're not."

"But I scared Elsie, I think."

"Maybe somebody scared you first."

She considered this. Did Problem Kids come from Problem Adults? Or could they be problems all on their own? She said, "I think I did something bad."

Finally, Jack faced her. A simple twist of the head could now appear strained on him. His eyes met hers, then wavered. "I did, too," he said, his voice thinning. She saw a hint of Serious Daddy in his eyes. She saw a face that held back some other thought.

"I think Daddy's gone because of me."

Jack stood up. "Annabel." Suddenly she knew what her brother was holding back. He was going to jump on the bed like she used to do with Fun Daddy, who'd land on the mattress like a tsunami wave, until Māma would rush into the room and tell him that he was crazy, the ceiling fan was spinning, and did he want their daughter to lose her head?

But no, her brother knelt down by the bed. He was more like Sad Daddy, a version that sometimes came out of nowhere and took over for the rest of the day. Sad Daddy never played games with her, but Sad Daddy was better than No Daddy.

Jack pressed his forehead to the edge of the mattress. "I'm sorry," he said to the mattress. She watched him for a while like that. When she tried to touch him, he patted her hand away. "Dad should be here," he said. "Not me."

After another minute, Jack joined her on the bed. He acted as if he had not been crying, and Annabel acted along with him. She went back to drawing in her notebook, which lay open on his bed. He took note of the doodles.

"Dad's not gone, you know," he said.

"He's in China."

"That doesn't mean he's gone."

Her brother had lost the alertness on his face. His eyes were tunnels. Māma had taken him to the doctor as well last week, though nothing had come out of it. When Annabel looked at Jack, she didn't know whether to think *sick* or *sad*.

Daddy had told her stories where sadness was a sickness, where people in China—and only China, she believed—could die of grief.

Jack looked closer at her notebook. A frowning stick figure filled the page, legs and feet planted at the bottom, one arm raising a giant sword to the sky; in the middle of the page, where the straight line of the body should have connected, there was a vast blank space.

"Oh," he said, still sniffling. "Where'd the rest of him go?"

Annabel clucked. "Nowhere. He's just separated."

She hadn't asked Jack what Jill Wu might have meant that day when she claimed her parents were *separated*. He probably would have told her not to worry, the code adults used for things Annabel wasn't supposed to know. Jack leaned forward as he turned the page, where the stick figure had become whole again, but smaller. He lay prostrate at the bottom of the page, Xs for eyes, his body open to the clouds. No sword in sight. "How'd that guy . . ." Her brother made a clicking sound and drew a line with his finger across his own throat.

"He's not *dead*," Annabel said. "He's sleeping."

The clouds filled up most of the page, big as the ones she remembered during summers, the view uninhibited by buildings or trees. Figures cut through the clouds, bouncing between them. Some were birds that looked like eyebrows. Others were creatures that Annabel had tried to pass off as angels.

She'd been trying to draw a separated man coming back to- gether, then falling asleep in an open field. Or had she been trying to draw a separated man sleeping in bed, dreaming of coming back together in an open field?

"He looks pretty dead," Jack said, and tilted the page against the light.

No more breathless days. No more fast-forwarding. Annabel Cheng, the subject of side glances and vicious games of telephone—or what others called Chinese whispers—was stuck. She whiled away the time at Logan by staring past the con- densation on the windows, willing her babysitter's tiny car to pull up at the curb. By 2:45 p.m. on January 23, Annabel was gone at the first glimpse of rescue. She zipped past Miss Katy and the mothers loitering near the front doors, and slumped into the front seat next to the original Problem Kid.

Charlene waved toward the school's entrance. She was wearing a tank top that barely clung to her shoulders, and her dyed hair seemed more orange than usual. She flashed An- nabel a mischievous smile. "Think she can see us?" she said. They watched Miss Katy dip her head, trying to X-ray past the heavy tint on the window. "At this moment, your teacher is trying to decide if I've kidnapped you in front of her eyes."

"I hate school," Annabel said, and kicked in front of her.

"Strong leg." Charlene shielded the glove box with her arm. "But I'm not sure how your mom would feel if I returned her bǎobèi in the form of air-bag-squashed guts. Also, stay in school."

"But you hate school."

"I hate people. Less useful."

Charlene hummed as they got on the road. Either she smelled like a skunk or the car did. In the past weeks, Annabel had spent so much time sitting illegally in the front seat that she could not tell the difference. Not that she minded the smell—it was just different. Around Charlene, different was not all that different. Charlene had gone, briefly, to college, though the āyís and shūshus talked about her as if she had never graduated from the realm of children.

"I can't wait for college," Annabel said.

Charlene laughed, and the car teetered slightly to the left. "What are you, six? Five?" She laughed again, more quietly. "You're a little sociopath, aren't you?"

With Māma not due home until later that afternoon, Charlene steered them back in the direction of Annabel's house. They'd usually find excuses to be anywhere but Huntington Villa, whether it was sneaking into the dollar theater, making stops at Sonic, or watching the Little League games at Russell Creek Park. Annabel liked to listen to Charlene talking on her phone, the way her voice pitched higher with her best friend, Brenda, as they exchanged mean impressions of a man Charlene was "seeing," how her laughter came from the belly and spilled in every direction, oblivious to the perked ears and eyes of people passing by.

"Are college people better, Charlene?"

Her babysitter's lips settled into a straight line. "Better is such a gross word." She glanced over at Annabel. "Someone bothering you at school?"

"Everyone hears things but me."

"Like . . . voices?"

"I guess. Why can't I hear them? Why am I the only one?"

"Because you're not fucking crazy." Charlene tried to smile. "My bad."

"That's okay, I know bad words."

"I mean, sorry that people can be such shitheads."

Annabel paused. A dream tape was playing in her mind again. A hand clutching her wrist, dragging her back home. *Quit it. I don't like it. Go away.* The voices she heard, no one else could. Was that not the definition of crazy? When the teachers saw Annabel's drawings of holes in smokers' necks or skeleton-looking kids, they always asked her where the scenes *came from.* She asked herself the same thing now.

Charlene stared at her for so long, the car could have been driving itself. She wanted to say something, Annabel could tell, but she needed to take her time. "Listen," Charlene said. "Everyone here knows how to talk, but that doesn't mean they know what they're talking about. I should know. I'm the Asian Mom Gossip Queen's Prodigal Daughter."

Apparently, even Charlene had learned the rumors about Annabel. How she was now the girl who gave other kids Indian sunburns. How she squashed bunnies with her own two feet. How she drank pig's blood. Miss Katy had taken her aside one day and asked if any of it was true. "Every culture is unique," she said. "I don't want to assume anything about yours . . ."

"Annabel?" Charlene was still looking at her. They had made their way back toward Logan Elementary, turning onto a familiar road that hugged the stone walls of her community. Charlene drove past the back entrance, past a man perched on a ladder, tugging the Christmas lights out of the prickly trees. "You know what I do when I need a time-out?"

"Break something?"

"No, you maniac. Donuts. A time-out . . . for donuts."

Ahead of them, Annabel's old school slipped into view. Bodies flashed between the slats of the playground fence, and a pair of hands walked its way across the monkey bars. In the parking lot, cars patiently maneuvered around one another.

"*This* way to donuts," Charlene said, and Annabel turned to look. In all the time that she'd gone to school at Plano Star

Care, Daddy had never taken her across the parking lot. A donut shop so close to an oily car parts store and squawking children, Concerned Daddy had grumbled. You would get all sorts of headaches.

Donuts were not the problem, Charlene insisted, they were the cure. She nudged Annabel out of the car, past the smell of gasoline and grease, and into the sweet, sickly scent that Yoon's donuts fanned outside. The air inside was oddly less cloying, the cafeteria-style tiles of the floor damp from being mopped. Charlene ordered a half dozen, glazed in a rainbow of options, and the Korean woman who waited on them threw in two kolaches because, as Charlene noted to Annabel on their way to a table, they were nicer to Asians.

"Well, at least the light-skinned ones," she said, snorting. "That reminds me. You call your people?"

"My people?"

"You know, your people. In China. For New Year's."

Annabel could only stare back. Who were her people? Charlene said, "Never mind," and set the box down on a table facing the parking lot.

Logan Elementary School must have let their people out earlier than Annabel's old school did, because parents were still filing through Plano Star Care. She recognized most of them, though she was beginning to forget which children they were attached to. Picking up kids at school, like squeezing your skull until your brains almost pop out, was one of those things that adults always do alone. At Plano Star Care it was Daddy who picked her up, and at Logan it was either Māma or Charlene. Annabel didn't know why this was a rule.

"Gōngxǐ fācái," Charlene said, and raised a neon-green donut in the air. She scarfed it down with an alacrity that could be heard. People were watching, but Charlene never seemed to feel the burn of another person's eyes.

A pair of adults emerged from a blue sports car in the parking lot and made their way toward Plano Star Care. Even from afar, the lanky figures and nice clothes instantly identified them. *Elsie's parents.* Annabel had not seen them since the Thanksgiving party, when they'd turned on her parents because Elsie had gotten scared and cried. It seemed unfair to Annabel, considering *she* was the one who'd made Elsie cry, and now a pulse ran up from the bottoms of her feet through her legs, and she found it impossible to stay still.

"Hey!" Charlene called, "Donuts, girl! Donuts!" Annabel was already out the door, bells chiming behind her. She was almost there! As she crossed the parking lot, she could see through the open door the potted ferns, the rainbow of hands she and the others had pressed to the wall. *My people.* Somewhere around the corner, both parents on their way to pick her up, Annabel's friend would be waiting.

Inside, the lobby smelled, as it always had, of spilled watercolors and disinfectant. Tony, a boy whose sneakers she'd once filled with spiky sweet-gum balls, raised a single, hesitant finger at her as he followed his mother outside. She could still hear the patter of the Louise-Deflieses' footsteps, the fresh voices of kids from the playground. Annabel was about to follow the sounds down the main hall, when a door on the other side of the lobby swung open.

It was Elsie, shaking the water off her hands as she stepped out of the bathroom. As far as Annabel knew, Elsie had still not learned how to go to the bathroom by herself. But here she was, no adults in the vicinity, walking with a bounce to her step, buoyed, it seemed, by her own sense of triumph.

Then she saw Annabel, and her feet stopped moving. Elsie's knees bent forward past her toes, as if she were a broken-legged chair on the verge of collapse. A red bun bobbed atop her head, but nothing on her face would budge.

Annabel waved. "Hi," she said.

The few yards between her and Elsie settled back into focus. There was the plastic cover slipping off one corner of a lunch table. The hum of the heater. In her pink boots, Elsie looked like she had her feet submerged in cotton candy. Maybe they were stuck to the floor, and that was why she wasn't moving.

Annabel couldn't wait any longer. Back were the recesses where Elsie followed her so closely she hadn't realized Annabel was leading her in circles. The field trips where Annabel would pull Elsie away from the other kids, giggling as they paraded in a world where no one watched over them. The comfort of having an audience that always believed her words. Her constant, her one constant.

She walked toward Elsie. Before she could get there, the girl flinched, and something like an answer to a test clicked on her face.

"Stop it! Don't come near me! Step—back!" It was not so much Elsie's words that shocked Annabel but their volume. Elsie had raised a stiff arm forward, the bright, white palm erect in Annabel's direction. There was something so un-Elsie about the gesture that for a moment, Annabel looked around to see if she was copying someone else. "Back off! I mean it! One more step and I'll scream!"

But Elsie was already screaming, and within seconds her parents had found them. Miss King tailed behind. From the entrance, Charlene hurried toward them, the lid of the donut box flapping. There was a blur of bodies and shrill voices, a pause when the adults recognized Annabel and spit out her name the way judges said *Guilty!* on TV. Tears glistened on Elsie's face; her daddy wiped them off with his hands. Strangely, each time after touching Elsie's face, he touched his own, feeling for the skin under his eye, and his bottom lip.

Before Annabel could get a better look, Charlene pulled

her back. Only after Annabel had been taken far enough from the commotion, nearly to the door, did she realize that she'd knocked Charlene's box of donuts to the floor. The other children and their straggling parents had all poked their heads into the lobby by then, their gazes following the trail of fallen donuts to Elsie's parents, who'd formed a wall in front of the bawling girl. "No means no!" Elsie gasped, before finally accepting the sanctuary of her mother's arms.

In the fragile quiet, the murmur of Elsie's parents trickled through the room. Annabel didn't know what words they were saying to Elsie, but the more they said it, the quieter the girl's sobbing became. She was too far away for Annabel to see every detail, only that Elsie's māma was embracing her, rocking her back and forth on the gym-tile floor, and that Elsie's face was pressed against other faces, merging with them.

The other families began to disperse. Annabel wasn't sure what to do, whether she should still stand there, encroaching upon a seemingly private moment, watching. Charlene no longer pulled her away, as if she, too, were caught up in the scene. Annabel watched Elsie, whose crying had simmered down to sniffling. She watched Elsie's daddy, who brought a hand to his bottom lip, the finger grazing there before he spoke. She watched him sing something, a lullaby, soft as the first pattering of rain. She watched until she couldn't watch anymore, until she had to close her eyes. Then she listened.

• • •

By the time Annabel's māma arrived, the parties who'd remained at Plano Star Care had retreated to separate rooms and corners. Once they were out of one another's sight, the tedium of waiting had overtaken the high emotions of the confrontation. Māma's entrance broke this equilibrium. Her panicked cries for Annabel—built up, undoubtedly, over the car ride since receiving Charlene's call—grated on everyone's ears, including Annabel's.

To Annabel, seeing Māma brought no relief. Her invective cut deep, from Elsie's parents to Miss King to Miss Dreyfus to Charlene, whose face, upon hearing Māma, was leached of some essential Charlene spirit. The Louise-Deflieses, with Elsie huddled behind them, mentioned something about a *restraining order* with the calm of a teacher reminding a child to clean up after herself. Before Annabel could ask what a restraining order was, Māma snapped back, so agitated her blouse came untucked from her slacks. As she paced in the lobby, her arms wild, Annabel caught a glimpse of the white lines crawling up and around her belly button, lines Annabel and Jack had supposedly given her. By now the lines were no more special to Annabel than the hair on Māma's legs, but displayed here in front of everyone, they looked like worms.

"I'm sorry," Annabel said.

It wasn't Annabel who should apologize, the adults kept saying, though they could not come to a conclusion as to who should. After much grumbling and back and forth, each side simply gave up. They wandered away from one another, keeping enough distance that they didn't have to say good-bye. When Annabel veered toward Charlene's smaller car in the parking lot, Māma pulled her away. "Like mother, like daughter," she said, within Charlene's earshot. "They say no, Elsie's parents did not report us. Okay, fine. Then who? Maybe Helen send us her dropout daughter because she is feeling guilty."

"Guilty?" said Annabel, but Māma ignored her. "Sorry about the donuts, Charlene!" Annabel called. Charlene was almost to her car by then, her shoulders slumped as if she were the one who was most sorry.

Inside the SUV, Māma spoke in a jumble of Chinese and English without looking at Annabel. The gall of those parents, she went on. So fucking concerned, they have to force the school to teach the children—five-year-old kids!—self-defense. First the school does all that good- and bad-touching nonsense, and now this. The only thing those children were going to learn was how to be scared. And a restraining order? Well, Elsie's parents had made their point. Driving home took a matter of minutes, but Māma's monologue spiraled without pause. "They want self-defense? Well, now they are going to *need* self-defense. I did not say that, Annabel."

"Fucking?"

"*Háizi*. What is wrong with you?"

"Nothing. But Māma—"

"Good."

When they entered the house, Jack's shoes were already placed neatly by the door. He joined them downstairs for a simple stir-fry dinner, and neither he nor Annabel complained that Māma had not defrosted the rice enough. The excitement of earlier had begun to wane, and Māma settled back into her resigned, maundering state of the past few weeks. If she spoke, it was to ask Jack to help her with the dishes, to gather the trash. She did not tell him about what had happened at Plano Star Care.

In bed, Annabel once again had trouble falling asleep. Sleeping had become more nerve-racking in the past weeks, because she felt as if she were being timed. At some threshold that Annabel could never predict, Māma would give up on waiting and leave her side. That night, before the knots in Annabel's head had loosened, Māma slipped away again.

Left alone, Annabel did not dream. She was aware of this, as she lay under the sheets. Or maybe her dream was simply this: Annabel, lying in bed, waiting to dream. She would not go so far as to say that she was awake. But when she imagined opening her eyes she saw an open door. When she imagined the carpet under her feet, she felt it.

Past the L-shaped hallway, Annabel found Māma in the living room, blue TV light pulsing over her face. Her head lay crooked on her shoulder. She did not stir as Annabel moved toward her. The unlit Christmas lights lined the counters and walls all seemed to be stretching toward the ground and into the TV and the humming video player, from which a pinhole of green light emanated.

Whatever the TV had been playing, there was now only a steady pulsing blue. The longer Annabel stared at it, the more she wondered if something else was going on inside the blue. Swirling images, hidden messages. If she could just see what she needed to see, she would know everything she needed to know. When Annabel turned back to Māma, the swirls followed her, now covering Māma's face.

The máojinbèi hung loosely to Māma's knees. Annabel drew the blanket over her nightgown. Māma's neck strained. She had a long, white neck, like a swan's, like Jack's.

Annabel lifted Māma's head, which rose with the pressure of a few fingers. She wedged a decorative pillow between the head and shoulder. Māma's breath came out stuttered, but she did not wake up. Annabel was still not certain if she was awake herself. If this was a dream, then she could let her legs take her wherever they needed to go. Another few breaths, and she was walking through the foyer, toward the front door. She stood by the door, looking at her warped reflection over the brass knob. Then she covered her reflection with her hand.

It occurred to her that she was not used to opening doors; people always did it for her. The doorknob was too cold in her hands, too big. With her other hand, she pushed the lever above the knob down, and there was the sound of a click. She was about to turn the knob when a voice sneaked up behind her, and a small yelp escaped from her throat.

"Hey. It's cold out there."

Jack stood behind her, in his pajamas. He looked back at Māma on the couch, brought a finger to his lips, and sidled up next to Annabel.

"You're awake," he said.

Hearing her brother say it, she became convinced that she was. She had to be awake to hear him in the dark. To smell his hair, a shampoo scent that reminded her of Christmas all over again. She had to be awake to hear her own voice.

"Gēge," she whispered. "Do we live in the future?"

He smiled. "I wish. That'd be cool."

"It's got to be true. In China, it's *still* New Year's."

"Oh, yeah." Jack considered. "I forgot."

Things could make sense if Annabel allowed them to. It can be hard to remember the past when you live in the future.

"Maybe that's why Daddy's not home yet," she said. "He's in slow time, and we're in fast time, and he needs to catch up. But he's on the way."

"Hmm." Jack glanced at Māma in the living room, then back at Annabel—or rather, at the door behind her. He took her hand, drawing her away from the door, and a shock of memory came to her. They had done this before, in another life.

"Or maybe we could get him," she said.

"Oh, come on."

"Don't you know how to get to China?"

Jack firmed up his lips. She wondered if he might be considering it, but then he let go of her hand and walked away. Watching him disappear around the corner of the hallway, Annabel thought about all the futures she had not arrived at yet, the pasts she had skipped over. Maybe that was why Jack was always reading books from the old times. Or why Māma was so busy making microchips that were supposed to change the future. Annabel could not know what had happened to her, or what would happen to her. So Jack and Māma figured it out for her.

As if on cue, Jack reappeared, with their jackets in his arms. He handed Annabel's to her and pointed to her puffy slippers, glowing behind his shoes by the door.

"But China's not cold," she said. "It's *burning*."

Jack reached behind her. "We got to get there first."

8

The ankle monitor, Liang's lawyer assured him, could not even hear his snoring. There was no secret mic inside the black slab, no camera the size of a pinprick. The Plano police department's budget was healthy enough to woo former news anchors and bored investment bankers from New York City, but Liang was not living in a multitrillion-dollar Cold War spy game. His job was to follow the rules. Do not call, text, or email the Louise-Deflieses. Do not step closer than a football field from their house. Do not visit bars, liquor stores, strip clubs, or Plano Star Care. Do not engage in any illegal or potentially illegal activity. Do not leave Collin County. Do not forget why he was wearing the monitor in the first place.

Liang would get used to the feeling soon enough, he was told. But who could know how the straps on the monitor refused to accommodate his bones, how after too much walking his foot would go numb from lack of circulation? When Nina or Kerry from the front desk knocked on the closet door and Liang called out that he was busy, they did not know that he was standing by the outlet next to his fold-up cot, charging. At YOUR Home Studios, Liang wore wool socks and jeans, but when he sat down the hems slid up, revealing the lump. Why was he always at work now, his young assistants probably wondered. Was that thing on his leg a strength-training weight? A massive ankle sprain? A tumor?

A *felon*, Liang called himself, even if Barry Cowgill from Cowgill and Cahoon, LLC, reminded him that being charged with a third-degree felony did not make him one. It was a new year for the police, with new opportunities to police. Unfortunately for Liang, the altercation at Montmartre had occurred on the beat of an overzealous rookie officer, who was now in contact with DFPS and was convinced that it further confirmed the earlier report about the incident at the Thanksgiving Day party. There was nothing Liang could do before the grand jury deliberation, but with some luck, the jury would see hurdles like his absence and the children's interviews and the drinking and lying and general recklessness, etc. within a larger context. The important thing for now was to remove himself from any context. Stop asking who'd reported him. Show up early to every meeting with Marcy Thomas. Be a model citizen. And count his blessings, Barry added, sipping from a hideous mug his daughters had painted for him. At least the restraining order didn't apply to Liang's own family, wasn't that right? Liang could drive back home right now—if he wanted.

Did he want to go home? Perhaps the better question was whether he had a choice. When Patty had picked him up at the station, she'd also brought a laundry bag of clothes and ordered him to stay away. So be it, he'd thought then, and moved to his studio to wait. Somehow, a month passed. The only times he'd seen his wife were for mandatory meetings with their CPS caseworker. No more Annabel hurtling toward him in the carpool lane, plopping into the backseat of his car as if into a ball pit at McDonald's. No more Jack glued to a book at the kitchen table, his hand searching for the nearby carrots and landing instead in hummus. There had been a carefully orchestrated phone call on Christmas Eve, one that left Liang holding a phone still warm with his family's voices, reeling. Maybe he should just show up at the house, he'd think every night, drifting from corner to corner of the empty studio. But Annabel was adjusting well to her new school, Patty had told him. Jack had even taken Liang's scooter out a few times with Marco Martinez.

What Patty hadn't said, not once: *Come back*.

If Liang's underpaid employees knew that he was living in the storage closet this whole time, they did not say anything, either. Nina probably found it harder to tackle her accounting homework without the cover of more customers. Kerry played his Game Boy less, though he still snuck in a few rounds when he thought Liang wasn't looking. Liang still scolded whoever was there for the day, for missing phone calls or not lifting their heads when a gaggle of teenage customers came through the door, but he also tried to engage his staff with passionate talks about the *true mission* of their humble photography studio: that through their service, ordinary people might live forever behind glass cabinets overlooking family dinner tables, that they might be venerated by those who came after them, like gods. To Nina and Kerry, though, portraits of regular people, portraits to be wept over by sons and daughters and grandchildren, were nothing more than souvenirs. Not to mention, they noted, Mr. Cheng didn't take pictures anymore. The whole point was that the customers could take them themselves, right? Liang could not convince them that this was only part of their business, the moneymaking branch that fed the more meaningful branches, but what did they care? They treated him like a nuisance. "We're all set here, Mr. Cheng," Nina would say, when he insisted on staying through closing. "Why don't you go home and get some sleep?" Kerry would offer. A question he'd been trying to answer all his life.

He was failing to sleep again when his wife called, late one night.

"Listen, Liang. Something is wrong."

Patty spoke in Mandarin, her voice thin and reedy, as if she were out of breath. The clock read 1:14 a.m. One more week until February. Surrounded by torn umbrellas and stained backdrops, Liang sat up on his cot, and it nearly folded in beneath him. Where was the light switch? Talking to Patty in the dark made him feel as if he were living in the past. He knew that whatever she had to say would keep him up.

"Qīng-Qīng. It is so good to hear your voice."

Her breath halted on the other line. "The children."

For a moment, he thought that she was going to tell him that his suspicions about Jack had been correct after all. That the boy had admitted to seeing Annabel bully Elsie at the party, that he had witnessed his father trying to intervene. Not that such an admission would make a difference. Annabel's fairly accurate account had not stopped Marcy Thomas from keeping the case open.

"I don't know what to do," Patty said.

No, thought Liang. Better she say nothing. Better yet, let the two of them blather about the blurry images taken by that rover on Mars, the Super Bowl, even Patty's upcoming birthday. Forget character witnesses, pediatrician evaluations, teacher meetings, plans B and C and D.

"The children . . ." she said.

Liang nodded, though of course she could not see the nod. He did not know what to be afraid of now. Why couldn't Patty finish the sentence?

"Talk to me," he said.

"The children," she said.

She had triple- and quadruple-checked the house. Tore up and down their street, calling out their names. Pounded on the Martinezes' and Crawfords' doors, frightening their neighbors as they knuckled their sleep-crusted eyes. Slack-jawed, they had told Patty no, they had not heard or seen Jack and Annabel. They seemed more frightened by the fact that Patty had lost her children than the fact that they were lost. That was when she knew she could not ask anyone else for help, last of all the police. Their case with DFPS was still open.

Liang was her only option, she said, now to his face.

There was no longer any time for such words to sting him. Liang climbed into the passenger seat of her Tahoe and they sped away from his studio, as inconspicuously as possible. While

Liang's attention was pulled every which way—any movement in the bushes, any long shadow—Patty sat clamped up in the driver's seat. She'd already looped around every last cul-de-sac in Huntington Villa before picking Liang up, and now she rattled off horrifying plans B and C and D. Hotlines to call. Search parties to organize. And though there were no signs of foul play, an Amber Alert as a last-ditch option. Did Liang know the original Amber had been riding her bike in Arlington, only forty or so miles away from here, when she'd disappeared?

"Qīng-Qīng," he said. "How did they get out?"

The car swerved to the right, screeching before it clipped the curb, then to the left, knocking Liang into her. Then they were back in the lane. If two children had been walking along the sidewalk, their five-thousand-pound chunk of steel would have flattened them.

"Qīng—!"

"I'm sorry. I'm sorry."

Patty was shaking. For the third time he offered to drive, and still she ignored him. Strands of hair clung to her cheek. From Liang's angle, she could have been twenty-five, fifty. There was a vague smell of something fried and electrical in the car. After one of their meetings with Marcy Thomas, Patty had told Liang that she might be pulled from the DSP project that had consumed her life the past year, yet when he offered to help pick up the children from school, at least, she'd insisted that she was perfectly capable.

A car slowed down next to them before passing. Maybe the driver inside thought Patty was drunk. Maybe Patty *was* drunk. How else to explain the children getting out under her watch? It was Liang who had not taken a single drink since he'd left their house. All this talk from Marcy Thomas about having to go to AA meetings was ludicrous. Marcy had even asked him, during one meeting, about his family history. She was no psychologist, the woman said. But she'd worked with enough families to know that certain behaviors have genetic predispositions. Though her job was primarily to evaluate Liang as a father, she understood that he was also a son.

"Our children are missing," Patty said now, in Mandarin.

She seemed to be testing out the words. Liang repeated them after her, in English. It was no use. There was no trick to make what was happening less real.

They were headed back in the direction of Huntington Villa. Legacy Drive was empty and slick with the last hour's rain. It had been only a drizzle, but if Jack and Annabel had been outside, they would have been caught in it. How long could they have been gone by now? Judging by Patty's estimates, it could have been thirty minutes, it could have been three hours.

When they passed a torn-up stretch of Independence

blocked off by DO NOT ENTER signs, Liang saw his children encased in the drying cement. When a cargo truck roared past, blinking right before turning left, he saw their blood smeared across the bumper, their bodies stored inside. He wanted to reach across the gearshift for Patty's hand and tell her what he was seeing. It didn't matter how she had lost the children, he wanted to say. They only needed to stop losing them. But both her hands were cinched to the wheel.

There had been a time when he could have touched her, for no other reason than simple curiosity, to see how a part of her felt. To do so now felt like a violation. If she allowed him to take her hand, who was to say that he would not crush it?

She slowed the Tahoe to a crawl. Along with Liang, she scanned the hopelessly vast landscape. Hedgcoxe was littered at this time of night with unidentifiable mounds: a cardboard box here, a backpack there. When he pointed out what looked like a coyote, Patty started talking about the ones at the nearby park. Picnickers had been throwing them so many scraps that lately they'd begun to lose their fear of humans. *The Dallas Morning News* had warned that if this went on, the coyotes could begin testing humans out as prey.

He had read that article too, Liang said. He had read it in his studio and laughed, because the writer had made it sound like the world was ending. In Plano.

They passed the Baptist church on Ohio, its digital billboard advertising their labyrinth lined with stones from eighteenth-century Scotland. They passed the four-way stop at Tennyson, where he'd witnessed at least seven accidents throughout the years. When they'd first moved here from Houston, Liang had imagined this city, like all places he didn't know, as empty. Now he saw it as full. Every car a possibility— for picking up hitchhikers and drunk fathers and husbands, for hit-and-runs and child abductions. A son was not only a son. A father was not only a father. A weed, Liang had declared to Patty, could not simply be a weed.

Then there was the moon. Tonight it was nothing more than a scratch in the sky. Were the children looking up at it, too? When he was a child, Liang had imagined his mother hiding out in the shaded parts, dodging the craned necks and eyes of those below her. He had spent so much time looking for his mother that he had not thought about what she could see from there. How much space she would have to take in from her perch, how big and incomprehensible it must all seem. The earth like a perfect blue globe. Every human as invisible to her as his children were to him now.

"Qīng-Qīng," Liang said. "The police. It's time."

He heard a hiccup, then an exhale. Patty glanced at him, glanced at the road. Finally, she turned left on Sheridan, toward home. They should not have gone out searching together, Liang realized now. He should have taken his Volvo and she should have stayed at home. He entertained a fantasy that the children had already made it back, and they were waiting for their mother and father on the front steps, breaking into a cantaloupe they'd filched from someone's backyard along the way. Maybe they wouldn't have to call the police after all.

They drove past the first concrete foundations of unnamed buildings. Industrial fences picked up where walls ended. When Liang spotted Plano Star Care around the bend, a burn seared his ankle. His skin tingled, as if the monitor had delivered an electric shock. That couldn't be right. Ankle monitors didn't carry the technology to listen in on their conversation, let alone to administer an electric shock. Liang wondered, with a sinking feeling in his stomach, if the DSPs Patty designed at work were inside his ankle monitor.

To his surprise, she turned into the Plano Star Care parking lot and nestled the car into one of the spots farthest from the streetlamp.

"We need to go," he said.

Patty switched off the lights. A dry swallow traveled down her throat. "I was in the living room, watching our old home videos," she said. "I was watching them, and I fell asleep, and they got out. I was right there, and they got out."

"Qīng-Qīng—"

"You aren't in those videos. Did you know?"

Of course he wasn't, thought Liang. He had recorded all the videos. "It's not your fault," he said. "You fell asleep. There is nothing wrong with sleeping."

Patty stared ahead. Or was she looking at the rearview mirror? Behind them, the moon arced over the prairie. A single paved path cut through the field, over the crest of a hill. At the end of the path would be Logan Elementary School: Jack's old school, Annabel's new one. Liang closed his eyes, tried to imagine the moon as brighter.

"I have this dream, sometimes," he said to Patty flatly, in Mandarin. "My mother is hanging from a roof beam in the old, communal barn. I stand over the straw floor and peer up at the white, swaying bottoms of her feet."

He could hear himself reciting the story, with the voice of one of those letters from the Plano Star Care teachers. He couldn't believe he was saying it.

"My grandfather told me then that she had fallen from the hayloft and landed wrong. An unfortunate accident. I remember my grandfather telling me about it more clearly than I remember seeing my mother, hanging from this great height."

"Liang—"

"My father told me she left us to live on the moon." He

opened his eyes to find that he was looking down at his hands. "He played the hero, always spurned by her. I don't think he was kind to my mother. He wasn't to me."

"The woman on the moon," Patty said. She, too, had inherited this version of the Cháng'é story. She probably remembered Liang's telling of it as sweeter, more quiet and melancholy than bitter. "She lives on the moon, with a rabbit for company," she said. "She lives on the moon, watching over us."

"Yes. Something like that."

"Hey." Patty looked at him now. She looked softer. "Are Jack and Annabel safe?"

"Of course. But first we have to go—"

"I mean, if we find them. Will they still be safe?"

"What do you mean?"

"Will they be safe—with you?"

So she had asked it. She was asking it. Not for him to come back, not that. What did she want him to say? That he had been trying to keep his family safe, the night he'd forced himself past the Louise-Deflieses' front door? That even as Elsie's mother retreated to a bedroom to call for help, and the blind Yorkie barked by Elsie's father's side, Liang had been thinking: *I am trying to keep my children safe?*

"I can't . . ."

Patty took his hand. "I need to hear it."

SIMON HAN

What he would never tell her, what she could not know, even from the police: at some point, Liang had cradled the back of Elsie's father's neck as if it were that of a baby. The man's coffee-colored pupils had wobbled. On their surface, Liang could no longer see his hands. He saw, instead, a reflection of Annabel. He saw Patty. He saw, clearest of all, Jack, who looked back at him not with fear but with knowing. He saw cheeks purpled, veins bursting, a face so distorted it resembled Liang himself. Even as he heard gurgling, Liang did not see his hands. He'd thought the gurgling came from the chocolate fountain churning on the kitchen counter above him and paid it no mind. It was only when he spotted Elsie peering out from behind a bar stool that he realized how hard his thumbs were pressing down on her father's neck. Blood threaded the man's teeth. The girl looked disoriented, not even there. Without thinking, Liang reached out to Elsie, but before he could touch her she fell on her bottom. He had only wanted to show the girl that these were gentle hands. Hands that could keep a person safe.

Patty was still waiting.

"Will they be safe—with you?"

There was the right thing to say, and there was the true thing to say. He sat with her in the thickening silence, trying to decide. Then, just before he was about to open his mouth, a different realization came to him.

"I know."

"You know?"

"Qīng-Qīng. I know where they are."

Patty had told him a story once, a story her mother had told her once, about two ghosts who fall off a bridge. The two ghosts are not actually ghosts but humans mistaking each other for ghosts on a foggy night. They realize their mistake only after they push each other off the bridge, after they're both on their way to becoming ghosts. Liang had laughed at the story then. Now he was pulling Patty out of the car, then across Sheridan, before she told him to stop. And in the middle of the road, she stopped.

"You're hurting me," she said.

Ahead of them, across the clover fields, stood the giant white-beamed soccer posts that marked the outer boundaries of Logan Elementary School. To the east of the playground was his intended destination. Leafless black willows shot out from the evergreens, their branches hooking onto the sky. After they caught their breath, Patty allowed him to lead her through the fields and tall grass, until they slid down a slope to softer ground. With her hand clasped against his arm, they stepped gingerly over gnarled roots. He could hear the drip-

drip of a natural faucet, the plunking of an object going un-derwater and not coming back up. Perhaps his sneakers were sinking. It was too dark to make them out.

Without much moonlight, Liang relied on smell: the damp-ness of the fallen oaks, with lichen and moss crawling over them. When was the last time he'd encountered a dead tree? It reminded him that the trees on his front lawn were living. He followed in the direction of the stagnant water smell, and Patty whispered from behind him that she did not want to go farther.

"Jack took me here once," he said.

"Really?" she said.

They walked over wood chips. Every few steps, they knocked against a stray rock, or what sounded like a soda can. Some-times he had to clear a drooping bough, careful not to let it whip back against Patty behind him. The adrenaline coursing through him made him almost numb to her hand as it slid down into his. He hoped he wasn't clutching her too tightly, though he could not tell who was clutching whom.

Finally, as they took about ten more steps around the edge of the bank, he dropped Patty's hand, just as she dropped his. Sprouting from the faint gleam of water was a lopsided figure slightly taller than Jack. Under the trees, the figure appeared deformed. The light was coming from a single slipper, floating on the surface of the pond.

How long did it take for Liang to realize what he was seeing? Maybe a matter of seconds—an instant—before instinct kicked in, and the picture focused for him: not some two-headed chimera, but two people, one carrying the other. Later, he would spend a long time imagining what had been in his son's head as Liang had barreled in his direction.

Annabel had fallen asleep in Jack's arms. The pond was not the sanctuary that the boy had remembered it to be. It was small and shallow; it was a dump. Maybe Jack remembered that afternoon with his father, how after the pond they'd come home and he'd forgotten to take off his shoes and left muddy tracks on the rug his father had steamed earlier that day. Why had he brought Annabel here?

Then a creature was coming toward them, roaring ahead with its arms swinging like battering rams, toppling everything in its path. A soda can ricocheted off its feet and flew into a tree trunk. Move, Jack told himself. Soon it would reach him and Annabel. Annabel! His little sister had forgotten how to breathe, sealing every particle of air inside her; she grew lighter in his arms, more weightless than a can pitched into darkness. Jack clutched her tighter as the creature rumbled ahead, stretching out its arms. Jack draped his body over his sister's. He crouched and turned her away.

The reflex passed as quickly as it had happened. Jack stood up again. Annabel had lost her other slipper. The hems of her pajamas were dripping with pond water. Jack's shoes were already soaked, the shoelaces undone. Liang lowered his arms. What could he do but watch? He had wanted only to collect his children, to protect his children.

Later, Liang would wonder whether Jack had recognized him from the start. Whether he'd shielded his sister in spite of that. Because even though he recognized his father, he was still afraid.

It wasn't until Patty caught up to them that Annabel finally sprang awake. She kicked out of Jack's arms and into Liang's, squeezing her father's neck so hard he had to pry her little fingers off him. The Velcro on her jacket sleeves cut against his cheek, but he did not mind. The first thing Annabel said was that she knew this wasn't a dream. She just knew it. The second thing she said was that she owed him so many kisses. She said it as if it was she who'd abandoned him. Over her shoulder, Liang watched Jack watching. Two months ago, someone had suspected that Liang was capable of hurting his own child. Twenty minutes ago, his own wife had asked him the same question, in so many words. No one but Liang had been wrong. He was capable. He was so very capable.

"Dad," Jack said. "I just—I wanted to show Annabel—"

Before Jack could finish, Patty had pulled the boy out of the water and into a hug.

Then Jack and Patty climbed the bank together, Jack holding the crook of his mother's elbow, guiding her. The gesture was so tender, it seemed outside of what Jack could deliver and what Patty could accept. Watching them, Liang felt himself floating. He would have made it to the moon had Annabel not clung on. It was the weight of her in his arms that tethered him.

"Dad," said Jack. "Dad."

It was Patty who finally spoke up. "What are you *thinking*?" she said. "Nǐ shénjīngbìng'a? Take your sister out here, scare us like this?"

"I just wanted to—"

"You *just* wanted to—"

"The beaver. I just wanted to show her the beaver."

Patty's breath caught. She seemed unsure whether Jack was joking. Her silence seemed to frighten Jack more. He went on about the beaver, the brown fur slick with water, how it had risen over there, on the other side of the pond. How he'd carried his sister into the water to get a better look. And then he'd seen it, climbing up the bank and scurrying past them with its whiskers to the ground, its flat, scaly tail dragging dirt behind it. Jack had never seen a real life beaver before, but he knew, he knew that it was one. If only he had a camera, one like his father's. The beaver had scurried in the direction from which

Liang had come. A shadow inside a shadow. He had seen it, he said. He had really, really seen it.

"*I* didn't see a beaver," Annabel said.

"You were asleep!"

"Beaver?" Patty said.

"Yeah, Mom. A beaver. You wouldn't believe it."

"I believe it," Liang said.

And now everyone was looking at Liang, in a new silence.

It was Annabel who broke it. "Who cares about a beaver?" she said, as she let herself down from Liang's arms. She had spotted his ankle monitor. She poked at it with a stick, demanded to know what it was. Was it a Bad Thing? Was it like an ankle bracelet? Why was it so ugly? Also, was Daddy coming home with them tonight?

Liang did not have an answer. Maybe he never would. Annabel's memories of his absence would grow and mutate and thicken into lumps, lumps that she would never be able to smooth out. And this lump fixed to her daddy's body, marking him as the hazard he would never cease to be: maybe she would always remember him like this.

But there was still the matter of the beaver. He said it again to make it true. He said it so that everyone, even the beavers, could hear. "I believe it. Of course. Why not."

9

One week later, on February 5—thirty-eight years after Patty had been born and eight hours before twenty-three Chinese laborers, picking cockles off the coast of Lancashire, would be caught by an incoming tide and drown—the Chengs were on their way home. Liang and Jack in one car, Annabel and the woman of the hour in the other, skirting traffic by taking the local roads. Here were the fields where horses still grazed and parking garages in construction threw down their shadows. Here was Plano, its Spanish name bungled by a white physician who was going for "plains" and arrived instead at "flat." Here was a road named after Colonel William G. Preston, who'd commanded a supply post along the route, where cattle herded to Midwest markets crossed paths with dilapidated covered wagons trundling south into the exaggerated promise of Peters Colony. Here were corn and wheat fields replaced by corporate parks and, one day, Toyota North America, which would transplant its headquarters from Torrance to the glee of every California-hating Texan. Here were car models more Googled than the tribes they were named after. The Paleo-Indians who'd left after drought. The bison and black bears and turkeys and gray wolves. The blackland soil. The hackberries, pecans, and bois d'arcs that for the most part now lay in the ground, buttressing the asphalt across which Liang drove his son.

Here was Jack in the passenger seat. It was no small thing. Liang tried to drink in the sight of the boy without giving himself away. To see Jack from the corner of his eye was to see something incomplete, filled in by memory and inspiration. Better to look at the road. The eye, after all, works in the same way as a camera lens. Position your subject as far out as possible, and you can focus on the subject while discerning, with clarity, the environment around him. Bring the subject closer, and the world around him blurs.

Maybe that was why Liang would always have trouble meeting his son's eyes, Liang's future therapist might suggest. To see Jack was to reenact the loss of Liang's mother, the unreliability of Liang's father. A state of detachment passed down from father to son-turned-father to son. What else? Rejection, perhaps. Blame. Unexamined trauma. Who could say? Only in America are people naïve enough to name everything they see. A few days before, while Liang was still working up the courage to move home from his studio, Jack had admitted, over the phone, to keeping Annabel's sleepwalking a secret. Liang could have responded, *Is there something else?* He could have said, *It's okay if there is something else.* He could have said it, or not. Always, there was the possibility of not saying it.

Jack, who was also discreetly watching Liang, was thinking of other possibilities. He had graduated from conjecture. His father was here. He was more concrete than the cake in Jack's lap, thicker than the strawberry frosting smeared against the box's plastic window. If he wanted, Jack could lift the cake out and flatten it over his father's face. He could draw a mustache over his father's lip. *Who are you?* he could say. *Who am I, if I can't be you?* Jack could do all this, or he could not. Restraint could be a kind of love. It would always bear the possibility of more love. As Jack peered through the rear window of the SUV in front of him, through the spaces between laundry bags and bobbing balloons, he kept his hands on the cake box. He turned to look at an old cemetery surrounded by luxury condominiums. In a couple of months the newest families of Plano would be out there, posing for pictures with the bluebonnets.

In the radio-murmur quiet of the Tahoe, Patty checked the rearview mirror and saw nothing. No daughter. Only the top of an empty seat. Imagine, she thought: a world where the seats in the rearview mirror stayed empty. Where it was okay to look at those seats and say, *May you never be filled.* Beyond the empty seat, through the spaces between the laundry bags and the bobbing balloons, Liang and Jack looked pensively in her direction. The moon and the sun, together at the same time. Perhaps their foursome would always appear a contradiction to others. The family who was allowed to stay together by the tenuous strings of a *safety plan.* As Marcy Thomas had outlined the other day, Liang would be required to take anger management classes, see whatever "experts" Patty's health insurance covered; Patty would meet with a permanency-planning supervisor to discuss, ridiculously enough, work-life balance. Meanwhile, the other parents wouldn't need to go to dinner parties to get the better dirt; in seconds, they could go on a DSP-powered computer and find, with a simple court records search, that Liang was still waiting to be indicted for felony assault. *Husband, father, felon.*

"Annabel," Patty called to the rearview mirror, but the spell failed. The girl did not suddenly materialize. There was a time when Patty had sent electrical power from a primary coil to a secondary coil without the slightest physical touch. She'd created electrical fields others could not see. Maybe the closest she would get to becoming a magician now was to drive to Texas Semiconductor earlier than anyone else and dream up code that would make something smaller than the palm of her hand respond, in an instant, to touch. This was the future that she could control—could speed up. She would apologize to Brent for failing to respond in a timely manner to their clients' last-minute function requests. She would apologize to Raj, Karl, Chethan, and Pranav for pulling them away from their families in order to avoid further delays in production at the Taiwan fab. She would duck her head down and work. She would do this until there was a more just way forward. But first, she needed to look back. Where was Annabel? When Patty turned around, she saw the girl was lying across the seats, asleep.

When Annabel closed her eyes, she'd imagined herself in China. She could smell the rot already, the fires fed by corpses. Whatever other people thought of China, it was the one place that yoked Jack, Māma, and Daddy together. She would have to be brave to burrow deep enough to slip to the other side, to find the pieces of them that she did not carry.

Many years later, stepping off the plane by herself in Beijing, Annabel would wonder why she'd kept waking up during the fifteen-hour flight. Why she'd felt so out of breath, as if she'd hiked a mountain in her sleep. Lǎolao and Lǎoye and one of her jiùjius would be waiting by the bus to Tianjin with a big sign they'd later translate for her: WELCOME BACK. But where had she been trying to return to? This massive place had never been hers to mine for answers. Every night in her mother's family's sweltering apartment on the outskirts of Tianjin, she would lie awake, imagining herself back in Plano.

Not the Plano where she insisted on living after college, with its trendy cupcakes and mall-size gyms and burgeoning music festivals, but the Plano she clung to in fading memory. Neighbors' backyards you could see into. Ancient trees circling a pond. A pair of glow-in-the-dark slippers, floating like boats. Perhaps she'd sleepwalked through those days, just as Jack had claimed, those memories pitched to the realm of dream.

In the car, Annabel's five-year-old self snored. She snored past a Marriott and an overnight warming station. She snored past the houses where Charlene Huang and Elsie Louise-Defliese lay hidden. She snored past dreams of a hand yanking her back, another hand yanking her forward. Now a third hand met her arm. Lifted her arm and laid it back over her seat. When she peeked outside, clover fields blurred by. Annabel would remember the drive like any other: a thing you did in Plano.

Across the clover fields, beyond the tall grass, in the enclave that none of the Chengs would ever desire to visit again, a boy was shaking a soggy, matted slipper in front of a girl he secretly hoped to marry. Hearing the girl squeal, their teacher rushed over and seized the slipper from him, only to drop it in disgust. Something needed to be done about this sorry excuse for a pond, the teacher thought. Right now, it was better suited for hiding bodies than teaching children about Plano's natural wonders. Who knew what diseases teemed in every nook and cranny that her second graders insisted on poking their hands into? There was Vu again, shoulder to shoulder with Cassandra as they looked down at the slipper. He wasn't poking the slipper so much as petting it. They were both crying.

"Okay, I'll bite," the teacher said, crouching down to meet the children's eyes. "What's wrong?" With two fingers, she picked up the slipper, warily, by the end. Though heavy with water, the slipper was small. Made for a child. It pulsed with a faint light.

"Mrs. K, what happened to the other one?" said Vu.

"Mrs. K, what happened to the *feet*?" said Cassandra.

Here were the children, with their dirtied hands and wet faces and strangely beautiful questions. Watching them, Mrs. Karjalainen almost wanted to join them in their crying. It had been a long year. She'd cleared out her dead sister's house in Tulsa, and her husband was always flying back to Finland, and sometimes all she had were the children. Not only the children currently tearing up this piss-poor excuse for a nature preserve, but the children who came before them, who'd stamped leaves of another time into the mud, who'd broken their nails trying to scratch their initials into the bark. They wanted to be firefighters and doctors and dragon tamers and the pilots who write messages in the sky. They wanted to be mothers. They wanted to be fathers. Some wanted parents who talked to them instead of setting them in front of a TV. Some wanted parents who left them alone instead of yelling at them or, say, throwing a mug of steaming coffee at their faces. Some would be content to have any parent at all. None of the children were her own, yet when she talked about them to her friends, she said *my, my, my.* Now two of them were waiting for her to make everything right, to transform this smelly, battered slipper from a prop in a scene of tragedy into something else.

Mrs. Karjalainen supposed she would have to do what she did best, which was to tell a story about it. But where to begin?

On the other side of the clover fields, Jack Cheng gasped.

"Candles," he said from the passenger seat. "We forgot candles."

Turning to look at him—to really look at him—for the first time that day, Liang saw the sheet cake in its precarious packaging, held together by Jack's sturdy hands. How long had it been since they'd celebrated Patty's birthday with candles, let alone a cake? "I think we have some at home," Liang said. "We can reuse the three from Annabel's birthday."

"But the three wasn't from Annabel's birthday. We got it for your birthday, and reused it for her birthday."

Liang chuckled. Jack's memory would never fail to astonish him. "You are right. The candles are much too old. I will buy more later. How about the trick ones making sounds? *Boom-boom!*"

"That sounds like a bomb, Dad."

"*Kshhhh.*"

"That sounds like opening a Coke."

There was laughter in the car now. Maybe there was laughter in the car in front of them, too, Liang thought. There was the outline of Annabel's head emerging over the top of the seats, the girl peering back at him. There was Patty's arm reaching toward Annabel's head, a swift gesture that was likely an order for Annabel to sit back down and put on her seat belt or else.

When Patty had picked up Liang at the Houston airport more than decade ago, she'd gestured to him in the same way. This was not China, she said, and motioned for him to buckle up. Patty had no license; she'd borrowed a classmate's car. Her apartment was only ten miles from the airport, but she drove with her chin nearly touching the wheel. Cars honked as they peeled past her, and she glared at them, her eyes arriving, at the end, on Liang.

Soon the car ran into standstill traffic. The drive began to feel like an extension of Liang's two plane rides. The edges of his wife's resentment sharpened. They still hadn't touched. Before he'd moved with her to America, before they'd made love, before they'd married, before she'd helped him sleep at night, every touch and response had already carried for them the flicker of danger. He felt as if he were encroaching on her space by breathing the air next to her. To see her in the car confirmed what he'd been trying to deny to himself for the six months since Patty had left for Houston: she had not wanted him to come to her.

He closed his eyes and thought about their son instead, who could focus on objects in front of him with the little camera of his eyes, and by then even crawl toward them. What was it like to see the world like that? He wanted Patty to see him like that.

What Liang had not anticipated, as Patty drove him back from the airport, was falling asleep. When he woke up, he was still in the car, parked in front of a brick wall. Patty was gone. Beyond her vacant driver's seat, a Black man was eating lunch in his Jeep, bobbing his head to his radio. Liang wandered inside the drugstore—a Walgreens—and asked the Hispanic woman behind the counter where his wife was. Only after she pointed to the back of the store did he realize how strange he must have sounded. He reached the bathroom, which was locked. He stood there, waiting to see Patty's face again when she opened the door. Would she berate him for following her—to the bathroom this time? He already imagined the question to come: Nǐ zài zhè'r gàn shén ma? *I am here*, he would offer back, *because I deserve to be here, too.* Even in Liang's imagination, his words sounded like someone else's.

For a long time, Patty did not come out. He suspected that she had heard him, from the other side, and was waiting for him to go. He lowered his forehead, as gently as possible, against the door. He could never afterward remember what he had said, with his head leaning against the door, but his lips had moved, and they had kept moving until a switch behind the door clicked.

When the door opened, the person he faced was not his wife. Perhaps in another life, but this woman, who looked Vietnamese, did not recognize him. Her eyes might have been kind, had they not been so leery of the person they were inspecting. He stammered an apology and stumbled back to the car. Patty was already in the driver's seat. For you, she said, gesturing to a plastic bag. There were Pringles, Bugles, Butterfingers, and Snickers. There was Gatorade *and* Powerade. She had wanted to have a meal ready at home, she said, but it was the end of the semester, and there had been too much work.

This was how it had always worked. Patty would move, and Liang would move in her direction. As he braked behind her at a red light, he resolved not only to move, but to move on. To Walgreens and Lowe's. To Michaels and Wendy's. To forgetting which stores had apostrophes and which ones didn't. To fitness clubs and Starbucks Bible studies. To driveway basketball hoops and backyard bounce houses. To garbage trucks carrying their smell elsewhere. To Janet Jackson. To the Dixie Chicks. To waking up to high school marching bands and going to sleep to the moon. To his mother. To 8:45 a.m. To the car in front of Patty's and the car in front of that car and the car in front of that car and the driver inside who was dazed with the shock of being alive on a Thursday at 8:46 a.m. and had forgotten to move on: move on.

When Liang honked his horn, Patty jumped in her seat, forgetting that she was not moving. What was Liang trying to accomplish, honking at a car that he could not see?

At last they arrived at Huntington Villa. Turning into their driveway, Patty pressed the remote clipped to the visor, and the garage door groaned open. Seconds later, the door creaked too early to a stop. Behind her, Liang must have pressed his remote as well. She waited for him to reopen the garage, just as he must have been waiting for her to do the same.

Was this their fate? They got in each other's way when they tried to stay out of it. They missed each other when they sought to collide. It hadn't been completely true that she had had too much work to have a meal waiting for Liang when she'd picked him up in Houston. Or rather, despite all her work, she'd spent hours making dumplings from scratch, but they had fallen apart in the boiling water. Walking up to the register with her arms full of snacks, she spotted, through the aisles, Liang at the back of the store. It looked as if he was bowing to the bathroom, pleading to the door. She stayed by the counter and watched. From a distance, she could see Liang but could not hear him. She could not hear him, so she invented what he was saying, the words she needed to hear. In the years that followed she filled his mouth in that memory with other words, or no words at all. The Liang from that memory could speak beyond language. Every time in the memory, he gave her what she needed. She'd thought that day that there was a chance for them. Then the woman at the counter asked her if she needed help, so she checked out and waited in the car.

In their driveway, Patty waited for Liang, and he waited for her. And in all that waiting, Annabel, now awake, took advantage of the child lock Patty had forgotten to reenable and darted outside.

"Hi, I'm Annabel! My daddy's back!" Patty could hear the girl even with the windows rolled up. She switched off the engine and joined her daughter outside.

Annabel was waving across the street at two women in windbreakers. They stood side by side, each one partially hidden behind a shaded baby stroller. They looked at Annabel as if she were a passing plane. Neither of these women lived on Plimpton Court, as far as Patty could tell. Or had the Brenners had another child? She could not recall the first name or the face of the Brenner woman, who lived a few houses down from them, only that she was friends with the Crawfords—the Crawfords, who might have heard about Liang from the Martinezes.

"Hello? Did you hear me? My daddy's back!"

"Háizi. Stop it."

In unison, the women unbraked their strollers and continued on their way, as if Annabel had not spoken. It took effort to be indifferent to a five-year-old girl's good news. Patty had an impulse to run across the street and overturn the strollers. But Annabel acted first. She tore a tuft of grass from the front lawn and flung it in their direction. "Shitheads!"

Shitheads. Another melding of two words Patty understood apart but had never put together. Now Annabel was kicking their mailbox; she would have knocked the cake out of Jack's arms behind them, if their jīn gǒu had not had the presence of mind to turn aside. Behind Jack, Patty could see Liang standing in the driveway, his hands fidgeting with his car keys. "Hey shitheads!" Annabel announced, now to the entire street. "My daddy's back!"

Jack watched Annabel, her eyes restless, bouncing from

house to house. How many people were behind those windows, watching back? When his sister took a second to catch her breath, Jack leaned down to her. He held the clear window of the cake box toward her. "See the palm trees? Don't you want to be at the beach right now?"

A beach would have been better than a pond. If he had taken Annabel to a beach, he could have laid her on the sand when his arms tired. They could have fallen asleep, not worrying about a thing, and woken up to the most delightful dreams.

One day, Jack would leave the house on Plimpton for good, and Annabel would think of him as someone who'd managed, back then, to be a witness to it all. When she would remember her father moaning in his sleep, or a woman like a cop, snooping in their house, or herself and Jack running off at night—had they really done that?—she would call her brother.

It happened, Jack.

Oh, I know.

But Jack?

Yeah?

What were we running from?

Even now, as Jack teased out the most beautiful description of all the different flavors beneath the beach-themed frosting of the cake, Annabel wondered how her brother knew so many things. He had lived entire lives before her, and entire lives after. It was as if he were still living all those lives now, lives from different times, and the same time. Even after she came home from her trip to China, Annabel would understand that there were lives she would never know, in her brother, in her parents. And this would scare her.

But for now, the family was moving on. Patty had taken one laundry bag of Liang's dirty clothes and the cake from their son, and she was crossing the lawn onto the cobbled pathway to the door. Jack and Annabel flanked her, balloons anchored in their fists.

Liang followed, but not too close behind. Beyond the open door, the house sucked the light from outside. It swallowed Jack, then Annabel, then the balloons that tapped against the upper frame before vanishing inside. A car took its time passing behind Liang. Somewhere, he heard a tap on a window. Planted in the middle of the pathway, his right foot, still outfitted with the ankle monitor, twinged. He tried to take the pressure off, but the pain volleyed to his other foot, his legs, his hips, his back. He ached. He ached, and then—he didn't know why—he stopped aching. He looked around. Patty had stayed by the door. She stood over the slanted welcome mat, steadying the cake and the laundry bag on either side of her. She looked at Liang in a way that made him want to hide his hands behind his back, because unlike her, for a single, blissful moment, he carried nothing.

She said, "Well, come in."

Acknowledgments

This book would not exist without the sure-footed guidance of Samantha Shea, my agent, and Becky Saletan, my editor. What a joy it is to have you both in my corner. Thanks to the teams at Georges Borchardt, Inc. and Riverhead Books for taking such good care of my work.

This book would exist only in the future tense without the gift of time and space from the following institutions: Vanderbilt University, the Tulsa Artist Fellowship, MacDowell, the Toji Cultural Center, and the Sundress Academy for the Arts.

This book carries the mark of all my teachers. Special thanks to Nancy Reisman, Lorraine M. López, Lorrie Moore, Tony Earley, John Keene, and Mia McCullough.

This book is indebted to Sasha Martin, Lisa Wang, and

ACKNOWLEDGMENTS

Meng Jin, who waded through entire drafts and helped me discover new pathways; to Lee Conell, Anna Silverstein, Marysa LaRowe, Jesse Bertron, Keija Parssinen, Morgan Holmes, Jennifer Latham, Randall Fuller, and Brett Warnke, who read excerpts and encouraged me to keep going; to my Northwestern, Vanderbilt, and Tulsa Artist Fellowship cohorts, who gave me the camaraderie that I sorely needed as a writer. Thanks to Francis D'Hondt, Yoonie Yang, Matt Tong, Susan Xu, and Jessica Lin for being early supporters; to Anna Badkhen, Rilla Askew, and Katie Freeman for mentorship and advice; to Clark Birdsall, Elizabeth Hocker, Karinda Smith, and Tina Johnson for help with research.

This book honors my family in America, China, and Korea. 感谢您们对我的支持和关爱。사랑으로 응원해주셔서 감사합니다. Little Fish, your support has never wavered. Aurelia, you continue to inspire me. Mom and Dad, you built a home for me in this world and let me play in it, even when my ways were not quite what you were expecting.

Chanhee, your stubborn belief in me is everything. This book is for you.